Horsefeathers' Mystery

Dandi Daley Mackall

SAINT LOUIS

Horsefeathers

Interest level: ages 12–16

Scripture quotations are taken from the HOLY BIBLE, NEW INTER-
NATIONAL VERSION®. NIV®. Copyright © 1973, 1978, 1984 by
International Bible Society. Used by permission of Zondervan
Publishing House. All rights reserved.

Text Copyright © 2000 Dandi Daley Mackall
Published by Concordia Publishing House
3558 S. Jefferson Avenue, St. Louis, MO 63118-3968
Manufactured in the United States of America

Library of Congress Cataloging-in-Publication Data
Mackall, Dandi Daley.
    Horsefeathers' mystery / Dandi Daley Mackall.
        p. cm. — (Horsefeathers)
    Summary: Sixteen-year-old orphan Scoop, a gifted gentler of
horses, does not believe that racing is good for horses, but
becomes involved with the sport after she and her coworkers
agree to stable and help train a special filly.
    ISBN 0-570-07128-3
    [1. Christian life—Fiction. 2. Horses—Fiction. 3. Horse rac-
ing—Fiction. 4. Orphans—Fiction. 5. Handicapped—Fiction. 6.
Brothers and sisters—fiction.] I. Title.
    PZ7.M1905 Hn   2001
    [Fic]—dc21   00-011892

1 2 3 4 5 6 7 8 9 10   09 08 07 06 05 04 03 02 01 00

For Matthew and Moby

Horsefeathers! Where's that brush?" I kicked up the straw I'd just spread neatly over the stall floor. "Carla! Have you seen the new brushes? Mr. Fitzsimmons will be here any minute!"

If Mr. Fitzsimmons liked what he saw, Horsefeathers Stable would be boarding its first race horses—nothing permanent, but for the couple of weeks around the County Downs races.

Carla and I had been in our own race all morning to get Horsefeathers Stable as fit as a Thoroughbred. We'd spent the whole, sizzling-hot morning cleaning stalls and sweeping out the barn. Only Maggie's white horse, Moby, and my beautiful black Orphan were left to groom. And now I couldn't find the brushes.

Carla had Moby in the cross ties a couple of stalls down from Orphan and me. Realizing that she might not have had her hearing aids in, I screamed, "Carla! I need a brush!"

"Easy, Scoop," Carla said. She and Moby

appeared outside Orphan's stall. Moby sneezed and draped her head across Carla's shoulder. "I don't have the brush." Carla's speech is impaired, so it sounded like: I don' ha buhsh. "I was going to ask you for the comb," she said, scratching Moby's chin. "Moby must have been swishing flies in a briar bush. Just look at her tail."

"Stay, Orphan," I commanded, hurrying out of the stall and around Moby to the tack box. I ferreted through old lead ropes, a hackamore, lunge lines, horse shoes, old rags, and even older brushes.

"Where are they?" I asked, slamming the lid to the tack box harder than I should have. "I emptied our Horsefeathers' checking account on those brushes, Carla. Jen almost killed me." Jen, our treasurer, watches every penny that comes in ... and goes out.

"Where is Jen anyway?" Carla asked, picking at the burrs in Moby's long, white tail.

"She and Travis drove by earlier. Jen had a doctor's appointment in Kennsington." I checked Cheyenne's and Angel's stalls for the missing brushes. The fresh straw smelled sweet, and I wished I could calm down and enjoy it.

"Where's Maggie?" Carla hollered, as I paced down the stallway, hoping the brushes would appear.

"Ballet practice. She said she'd get here as

soon as she could. I just hope she makes it before the Fitzsimmons people get here. Maggie could charm them into leaving all of their horses with us."

The last stall didn't have the missing brushes. But after checking it for the thousandth time, I decided it could use an even thicker floor covering. I hoisted two armfuls of straw from the mound at the back of the barn. The straw scattered like my little brother's Pick-Up-Stix, then sent dust dancing in long sunbeams. "Those race horses are going to need the softest floor we can give them," I said, brushing off the straw that stuck to my sweaty arms.

"Are you sure about this, Scoop?" Carla asked. "Are race horses what we're all about at Horsefeathers? I thought we were supposed to be the home for the backyard horses. Isn't that why you started the stable in the first place?"

Ordinarily I would have agreed with her, but we needed the business. To be honest, it was more than that. I wanted the boost in reputation Horsefeathers was bound to get from stabling some of the best race horses in our part of the state.

"We've gone over this a million times, Carla," I said, giving up and grabbing a beater brush from the tack box. Half the bristles were missing. "I don't like horse racing any better than you do. You know that. It's just ... well ...

you should have heard Mr. Fitzsimmons on the phone. He couldn't say enough good things about us, about Horsefeathers." Mr. Fitzsimmons of Fitzsimmons Racing Farms had called me that "teenaged horse whisperer I've heard so much about."

"Just think, Carla," I went on. "Out of all the places he could have boarded his horses for the County Downs races, he chose us."

"But still, Scoop," Carla reasoned, "they're high-strung, temperamental race horses."

I really didn't want to go through this again. We'd had the worst fight ever at our Horsefeathers meeting over the Fitzsimmons offer. But Carla had been outvoted fair and square—3 to 1, with Jen and Maggie on my side.

"It's not like we're getting into training race horses or anything," I said. Orphan nickered and nuzzled me when I rejoined her in the stall. "Besides, they're going to race these Thoroughbreds with or without us. Maybe I can help the poor horses not to be so frightened so racing isn't so traumatic for them."

Carla didn't say anything, but I knew she still disapproved. She pushed back the one strand of her shiny, black hair that was out of place. All of my hairs were out of place. The braid I'd started out with this morning had somehow come unbraided, leaving wavy, dark, renegade hairs everywhere. As always, even though Carla had mucked as many stalls as I had, she looked glamorous. Her Levi's didn't have a speck of dirt on them, and her green, cotton shirt wasn't soaked with sweat like my T-shirt was. She'd even managed to keep her tall, leather boots clean.

It was easy for Carla to turn down the offer to board race horses. She had plenty of money, and her horse already had a super reputation as a champion American Saddle Horse gelding. As long as Horsefeathers had a stall for Buckingham's British Pride—who was known to be pretty high-strung and temperamental himself—what did she care about Horsefeathers' reputation?

But I cared—more and more lately. I was tired of feeling second-class, like Horsefeathers was really just a barn, a joke to other stables like the Daltons.

"Anyway," I said, my voice sounding whiny even to me, as I kept brushing my mare. "Once they see the place, they probably won't leave their horses here. Horsefeathers isn't exactly what they're used to."

If Maggie had been there, she would have taken the cue and launched into cheerleading mode: *Of course, they'll want to stay at Horsefeathers, Scoop! Why wouldn't they want to stay with the best horse gentler in the whole wide world?*

Not Carla. "Maybe you're right," she said.

9

"When are they supposed to get here, Scoop?"

"Mr. Fitzsimmons said Saturday morning. I wish I'd asked him what time, but I didn't want to seem too anxious." It was no use trying to smooth Orphan's coat with the old brush. "Horsefeathers! I hate this brush!" I said, tossing it aside and resorting to my fingers to press out the rough, wavy ridges the stupid brush left on Orphan's coat. "Did you even get to see the new brushes, Carla? They're awesome."

"Are they natural wood, kind of white?" she asked.

"Yes! Where did you see them?"

"B.C. had a white brush this morning," Carla said. "He was brushing Misty with it."

"Figures!" I said, tearing out to the paddock. Orphan followed me, anxious to check on the colt she'd adopted a couple of months earlier. The foal's mother abandoned him, and my big-hearted mare took over from Day One.

I spotted my little brother at the far end of the paddock. B.C., short for "Bottle Cap," was messing with Misty, tugging on a rope he had looped loosely around the foal's neck. Misty, still covered with curly, gray baby fuzz, pulled back playfully, challenging B.C. to a tug of war. The colt looked more Arabian every day, with big eyes, pointed ears, and a well-defined jawbone. He was starting to carry his head gracefully, like his Arabian dam.

B.C. looked worse for wear than I did. He

was the one who needed brushing. His bushy, brown hair stuck out like porcupine quills. He was wearing the jeans Dotty had bought him, but they were fake jeans, too stiff and too blue, with yellow stitching. They looked too new, and Tommy Zucker wouldn't have been caught dead in them.

"What do you think you're doing, B.C.?" I shouted, stomping across the dusty paddock, wishing I'd taken time to water it down before the new people got there. "Don't put the rope around his neck!"

"It's really loose," B.C. said.

"Where's his halter?"

B.C. shrugged and didn't look at me.

"B.C.," I said, trying to control my temper, reminding myself that my brother's manic depression could grab him at any moment. He'd had two really good weeks—no crying jags or bouts of silence, and nothing too crazy. I didn't want to set him off. "What have you done with Misty's little halter?" My voice was level, strained, but not yelling.

He shrugged again. "I can't find it."

"B.C.!" I shouted, all my brother-sister res-olutions flying out the barn door. "I can't believe you! Dotty got you this colt so you'd learn to be responsible. And now look at you! You can't even keep track of Misty's halter. And where are my new brushes? Carla saw you with them this morning."

B.C. shrugged, not looking away from Misty. He took the rope off the foal's neck, and Misty trotted off, bucking once for good measure. Orphan walked up to the foal, and they rubbed noses, making little whinnies that sounded like a church duet.

"First, you lose my brushes, and now Misty's halter?" I didn't want to yell, but I couldn't help it. I clenched my teeth and sent off a quick prayer. *Okay, God. Please help me not to be so mad.* I still felt as angry as a caged Mustang. *Well,* I prayed, *please don't let me say anything I'll regret later.*

I took a deep breath. "Listen, B.C. I can't afford to get new brushes or a new halter. You'd better find them and get them back here fast. I mean it. What do you think Dotty will say when I tell her?"

"Don't tell her!" B.C. pleaded. "I'll find everything. I will!"

Telling Dotty was no big threat. B.C. knew as well as I did that Dotty, the aunt we live with, wouldn't have been mad at him if he'd lost everything we owned. But I knew B.C. never wanted to disappoint her. She'd been the only mother he'd had for over eight years, since he was 2 and our parents died in an explosion at the bottle cap plant.

"Okay then," I said. "But I need that stuff back today, B.C. Got it?"

"I'll find everything!" B.C. said. "I promise!

I will! I ... I'll find the white brushes and the little comb thing, and Misty's own special halter!" His voice grew louder and louder, the edge creeping in between his words. "And I'll never ever lose anything ever again and you won't have to tell Dotty and make her worry that something's wrong with me again and — "

"Okay, B.C.," I said, feeling bad that I'd taken some of my anxiety out on him. "It's okay. I know you'll find everything and put it all back. Dotty doesn't even have to know."

B.C. ran after Misty, and I wondered if he'd changed channels already and forgotten all about finding the lost stuff. I crossed the paddock back to the barn, where Carla was standing in the doorway.

"Oooh," she said in mock fear and trembling, "don't tell Dotty on me either." When I raised my eyebrows at her, she said, "I can still read lips, you know."

"I know," I admitted, leaning against the doorpost. "I kind of overreacted. But B.C. is so irresponsible. He drives me crazy."

"Misty sure seems to like him," she said.

"True." It was amazing how fast Misty and B.C. had bonded—two runts, two orphans. "They remind me of Orphan and me when Orphan was a foal. But you know we're still paying on Misty—one more reason we need this new contract."

A faint grinding sound came from the other side of the barn. "What's that?" I asked.

Carla cocked her head and tapped her hearing aid. "You're asking me?"

The noise, a churning like grinding truck gears, grew louder. "They're here!" I cried. "And Maggie's not here yet! Carla, what am I going to do?"

"Um, go talk to them?"

"That's what Maggie's for! You know I'm lousy talking to strangers. I'm not all that great talking to un-strangers."

"Un-strangers? You word wizard, you."

"Carla!"

"Oh, come on. I'll give you moral support."

I raced to the front of the barn and watched as a huge, black trailer bounced up Horsefeathers Lane. Carla stood behind me.

"How do I look?" I asked, trying to smile as the trailer drove up.

"Not bad, except for the straw in your hair." Carla plucked out long pieces of straw. "That trailer's carrying more than three horses, Scoop. There must be at least six."

"What? He only mentioned three horses. Can you imagine if he leaves us six?"

The trailer stopped, and the driver got out, a tall, thin, aristocratic-looking man who reminded me of Carla's father. His gray suit looked much too nice to wear on a long haul. "He's not at all like I pictured him," I whispered.

"What?" Carla whispered back.

A guy stepped out of the passenger side. He looked like a younger version of the driver—slim and dark with a long, straight nose. He closed the door, but kept one hand on the handle, as if he thought he might need to make a quick get-away. His gaze jumped from me, to the barn, and back to me. His mouth turned down at the corners. He squinted, although I was the one facing the sun.

"Father," he said, "I think we've made a big mistake."

2

I couldn't say a word. He thinks *he* made a big mistake? Carla was right. What made me think we could handle Thoroughbred race horses?

As the driver made a visual survey of the grounds and barn, I followed his gaze and imagined I was seeing Horsefeathers Stable for the first time, through his eyes ... and down his nose. What I saw was an old barn, gray with original barn wood, too much space between the wooden slats. Grandad used to keep 30 horses in this barn, but it didn't sag back then. The grounds weren't fancy—a paddock out back and pastures on the sides. Horses loved Horsefeathers; people, not so much.

"Hello? This is Sa-rah Coop." Carla pronounced each syllable as clearly as she possibly could. I wanted to hug her for being so brave. I didn't think anybody could have had trouble understanding her.

But someone did. "Huh?" asked the younger guy, frowning at Carla.

"I-I'm Sarah Coop. Scoop?" I said, taking a

couple of steps toward them. "Welcome."

~~~~~~~~~~~~~~~~~~~~~~~~~~~~~~

They didn't look like they felt welcome. The driver came around the trailer and shook my hand, his slender fingers barely touching mine. "Are you sure you're set up to handle race horses?" he asked. Orphan stuck her head over the paddock fence and nickered, drawing his attention. "Thoroughbreds?" he added quickly.

"I can work with any horse," I said, wishing Maggie could have chimed in with her convincing sales pitch. "I've had some experience with Thoroughbreds. Not racing them," I added quickly. "But you don't need me for that, right?"

"Right," he said slowly, his gaze sweeping Horsefeathers as if he were checking out a mine field before risking another step. "Listen," he said, "I don't mean to offend you, but this is not at all what I expected. I think my son may be right. We have made a big mistake."

"It may not look fancy here," I said, "but your horses will be better cared for than they ever have been. I know your trainer will work them out for races, but I can help—"

"How old are you?" he asked, cutting me off.

"16 ... almost," I answered.

"16? And what are you, one of the grooms?" He scratched his head and scowled at me.

"No," I said quietly. "I'm the owner."

The son snickered.

"The owner?" repeated his father. "And just who did I talk to on the phone?"

"Me."

"Come now," he said. "This is ridiculous! You are not the owner of Dalton Stables, and this is not the way your establishment was represented to me when—"

"Dalton Stables?" I asked weakly, my stomach feeling as if horses were trotting through it.

"Yes, of course. And your literature is very misleading. I see no indoor arena. I knew I should have driven out here and checked this out for myself. But honestly, Ursula usually has better judgment than this."

"Ursula?" I murmured, feeling things go from bad to worse. Ursula was Stephen Dalton's girlfriend.

"Ursula Langhorne? My daughter!" he barked. "She assured me I would not be disappointed in Dalton Stables. She's the one who talked me into boarding here for the races, instead of at the Downs."

"Did he say Ursula?" Carla asked, signing Ursula's name.

I nodded, feeling like I might throw up.

"No. I am sorry," he said, not sounding at all sorry. "This simply will not do. Dalton Stables is not appropriate for our line of racers."

"This isn't Dalton Stables," I said, my voice cracking.

"What?" he demanded.

"This is Horsefeathers Stable," I said.

His eyes and his mouth formed surprised circles. "It—you mean—you're—" He wheeled back toward his son.

"Horsefeathers?" his son cried. At the same instant, father and son burst into fits of uncontrollable laughter. "I thought it was—" "Then I saw—" "And she's the owner—" But neither of them could get out a whole sentence.

"I apologize," the man said after what seemed to me like minutes. "I'm Gregory Langhorne, Langhorne Farms, and this is my son Lawrence. We should have introduced ourselves right away. I am so sorry for the confusion. I-I guess we're lost."

"It's Ursula's fault," Lawrence said. "We should have known better than to trust her directions."

"Well, we won't make that mistake again," Mr. Langhorne assured his son. He turned back to me. "Lawrence and I live upstate. We only get down this way for the County Downs races every summer. My daughter lives with her mother not far from here. Perhaps you know Ursula?"

"Kind of," I said. Ursula and I weren't exactly pals. She and Stephen were two of the most stuck-up people I'd ever known.

"Perhaps you could direct us to Dalton Stables?" he asked.

I had half a mind to send them off in the wrong direction, but I didn't. "It's just a little over a mile up that way," I said, pointing beyond our back pasture. I told them the best way to drive there.

Carla and I watched them circle the trailer and drive off. When they turned, I could see the name on the side of the trailer: Langhorne Farms, 50 Years of Championship Thoroughbred Racing. We could hear them laughing all the way down the lane.

"It could have gone worse," Carla said as the trailer disappeared behind the row of hedge apple trees.

"Oh yeah?" I challenged.

"They could have been the Fitzsimmons people."

I'd almost forgotten about the real Fitzsimmonses. I couldn't imagine going through that whole scene all over again. "Horsefeathers, Carla! You think they'll be as bad as the Langhornes?"

"You're the one who wanted in with the racing set, Scoop," Carla said.

I gave her a dirty look and went back to the paddock to wet it down while we waited. Misty loped to meet me, his long legs stretching farther apart than they needed to, making him look wobbly. Orphan pranced up behind him. I scratched both of them behind the ears until their eyes closed to half-mast.

"You guys can always make me feel better," I murmured. I inhaled their honest, earthy horse smell.

"Want to go for a ride?" Carla asked. She'd taken Ham, her beautiful bay gelding, out of his stall and tacked him up English. He arched his neck and shifted his weight in anticipation.

"I wish I could," I said, yearning to just get on my horse and take off to the back pastures, escaping into the woods. "But I'm afraid I'll miss Mr. Fitzsimmons. You go ahead. But don't be too long, okay? I need you, Carla. I'm giving up on Maggie."

While Carla practiced Ham's gaits in the paddock arena, I pulled out the hose and watered down the area just enough to settle the dust. It probably wouldn't help though. Mr. Fitzsimmons was bound to be as disappointed in Horsefeathers as Mr. Langhorne had been.

No sooner had I wet the center of the paddock than Orphan and Moby trotted up. Moby dropped to her front knees, then folded her hind legs.

"No, Moby!" I cried.

But it was too late. The old, white mare plopped to her side and rolled over on her back, twisting and scratching in the mud. She looked so blissful I couldn't stay mad at her. Moby heaved herself all the way over, grunting with pleasure.

That was more than Orphan could stand. She nodded at me several times and snorted, begging permission to roll.

"Oh go ahead," I said. "They're probably not coming anyway."

Orphan dropped immediately in the moist dirt and followed Moby's lead, rolling all the way over twice.

"So I guess we didn't need those brushes after all," Carla shouted as she and Ham circled us at a canter.

Carla rode for a while. Then she waited around the barn with me while the horses romped in the paddock. After an hour, she said, "Scoop, I'm sorry. I can't stay any longer. I promised Ray I'd meet him back at my house. I'm already late."

"No!" I protested. "You can't leave me now, Carla."

"Scoop, face it. They're so late. They're probably not coming. Maybe they changed their minds."

"Maybe not. Maybe they just got lost," I suggested.

"And ended up at Dalton Stables?" Carla teased.

"Funny."

"Just remember, Scoop, if this racing thing doesn't work out, it may all be for the best. That's what Dotty always says."

I knew Carla was right, but it didn't feel all for the best. It just felt like another big disappointment. "Tell Ray I missed him mucking the stalls."

"Will do," she said.

After Carla left, I climbed to the barn roof, where I do some of my best thinking and praying. Under the shade of an overhanging oak, I closed my eyes and smelled bittersweet and alfalfa, mixed with the strong scent of green walnuts.

Why did I really want this job with the race horses? I hadn't gone out looking for it. They called me. But I had to admit it felt good that a big horse racing outfit like Fitzsimmons Farms would even know about me and Horsefeathers. Mr. Fitzsimmons had explained to me that he had a horse that was gate shy. The filly's fear of the starting gates on racetracks was keeping her from "graduating," from becoming a first-place winner. He'd heard about me from somewhere, but he didn't say where. I wondered if it was Twila from Cherokee Bend who had told him. He said he'd heard about how good I was in working with problem horses. I liked that. I liked it a lot, the idea that my stable had a reputation.

I wouldn't have traded my grandad's barn for a hundred stables like Dalton Stables, so sterile they didn't even smell like horse. But Dalton Stables had a reputation throughout the West.

They hardly ever had an empty stall, and Stephen claimed they had a six-month waiting list for boarders. I didn't envy Dalton Stables, but I wouldn't have minded a reputation like theirs.

Scuffling and nickering came from the paddock. I investigated and saw Cheyenne and Angel taking their turns rolling in the dirt and mud. It didn't matter. The Fitzsimmonses weren't coming. They'd probably taken their horses to Dalton Stables too. I wondered if Daltons would make room for them.

"Well, blow me down, and call me a leprechaun! If it isn't the wee lad, B.C.!" The unmistakable voice of Maggie 37 Brown carried to the roof. She was obviously working on a new Irish accent, another asset for her career as an actress. "And how be ye, laddie?"

"You talk funny," B.C. said, laughing at his favorite person on earth. "Talk more, Maggie."

I scooted down the slanted roof to where I could see them. Sure enough, Maggie and B.C. were talking in front of the barn. "Maggie!" I hollered down. "It's about time!"

They looked up, and I saw B.C.'s expression change completely.

"I have to go," he said, taking off at a run. It didn't take a genius to figure out that my little brother hadn't recovered my brushes yet.

"Scoop!" Maggie called, standing on her tiptoes in pink slip-ons and waving up at me. "I'll be right up!" Maggie's real middle name is really a number—37, her mother's lucky number and Maggie's birthdate: March 7—third month, seventh day. She changes her last name as often as she changes her clothes, in pursuit of the perfect stage name. Today she was obviously Maggie 37 Pink, in pink sweatpants and a pink sweatshirt.

"Aren't you hot in that get up?" I asked, pointing to her sweatsuit.

"In truth," said Maggie 37 with a twirl, "'tis hot indeed I be a-feeling this day, Scoop, love." Her words rolled out as musical as an Irish ballad. In one graceful movement she tugged off her sweatpants and shirt, revealing a pink tutu, with a starchy, stand-out short skirt. Her brown hair was gathered into a tight ballet bun on top of her head. "I saw Carla on the way here," she yelled up at me. "The real boarders still haven't shown up? Sorry, Scoop."

A loud bang sounded from somewhere out of my vision—a gun or a car backfiring. Maggie ran to the lane and stared down toward the main road. "Scoop! It's a truck pulling a horse trailer!"

Maggie leaned forward, shielding her eyes from the sun. I scooted to the edge of the roof and strained to see the trailer. Out of the corner of my eye, I caught a vision of something streaking from the barn. My brain clicked the image together, and I realized it was B.C.'s foal. Misty raced toward Maggie from one side. The trailer bounced up the lane toward Maggie from the opposite direction.

"Maggie!" I screamed, helpless as I watched colt and trailer headed for a collision, with Maggie in the middle.

3

M aggie! Misty!" I yelled. My foot slipped, and I slid down the roof, grasping at shingles that crumbled in my hands. I caught myself before sliding off the edge.

Below, Misty ran straight at Maggie. The trailer raced straight at Maggie. Maggie looked from one to the other. Her shoes skidded in the dirt. A horn beeped. Maggie toppled backwards. Brakes squealed. I screamed again.

From the barn came a loud whinny. Orphan ran out at full gallop, racing toward the foal. Behind Misty, Moby, then Cheyenne and Angel trotted, as if in parade formation.

The truck swerved off the lane, making the trailer thump to a halt. Maggie scrambled to her feet. She straightened her tutu and ran after the string of horses as they paraded in front of the truck—a blur of dirty horses followed by an African-American ballerina.

The driver jumped out of the truck. I yelled down at him, "Hi! I'll be right down! Don't go away!

I took the fast exit off the roof, jumping to the ground from the lowest sag. I landed on both feet, but my ankle turned as I hit the ground. Limping, I dragged toward the trailer as the driver closed the truck door and leaned against it. His eyes were wide as a spooked Piebald.

Hobbling around to his side of the truck, I stuck out my scraped and bloody hand. "Uh ... hello," I said.

He shook my hand, without taking his gaze off the ballerina chasing the string of horses. "Is ... is this Horsefeathers Stables?" he asked.

Misty made an end run around Maggie, kicked up his hooves and charged us. I knew he was just playing, but Mr. Fitzsimmons didn't. He slammed his body against the truck, dropping his keys in the grass. Orphan galloped behind Misty, sliding to a stiff-legged stop inches from us. Before I could grab Misty, he bolted around me to investigate the newcomer. The colt had a halter on again, but I still couldn't reach it in time.

"Ow!" screamed Mr. Fitzsimmons. "It bit me!"

His scream set off Cheyenne, the Zucker Paint. She reared and pawed the air a few feet from us. Maggie 37 reappeared, this time on the back of Moby, who trotted up between Mr. Fitzsimmons and me and then bowed on Maggie's command.

A boy hopped out of the passenger seat and hurried to his dad's rescue. He had to dodge Angel, Travis Zucker's Appaloosa, who had cantered up behind him, coming to check out what all the fuss was about. "Dad, are you all right?"

The man rubbed his forearm. "I'm fine. Should have seen it coming. You've got a good set of teeth on you, little one," he said, pretty good natured considering he'd just been attacked by a string of dirty horses, one ballerina, and a limping horse whisperer.

"I am so sorry!" I said, pushing Misty back and shooing away Cheyenne. "B.C., my little brother, has been hiding sugar lumps in his pockets. I told him not to. Misty was just looking for sugar. He didn't mean to bite you. And the gate—my brother must have left the stall door open, and the horses got out, and they were just being playful, but we're not usually like this, honest." I stopped chattering. I sounded worse than B.C. in manic gear.

Maggie slid off Moby as if it were all part of her ballet performance. "I am Maggie 37 Pink," she said, offering her hand to both speechless men. They shook Maggie's hand as they were instructed. "This is Sarah Coop, Scoop, of whom I am sure you have heard, since her reputation as the premier horse gentler has spread so widely. We would like to welcome you and your horses to Horsefeathers, where horses come first. We apologize for our temporarily unruly lot. But as you know, horses will be horses."

I sneaked glances at the two Fitzsimmonses, who had to be father and son. Father reminded me of the Nonius, a trusty Hungarian cavalry horse, sound, reliable, but not flashy. He looked like a regular, overweight, balding, middle-aged man. I liked his friendly smile. He was obviously no verbal match for Maggie 37, who would have been a performing Lipizzaner if she'd been a horse. Mr. Fitzsimmons was hanging on every word that came out of Maggie's mouth.

His son, if he'd been a horse, might have been a breed related to the Nonius, the Furioso—a sturdy, trusty horse, but more refined and better looking than the Nonius. The dad's grin tugged at the corners of the son's mouth. Already son had passed father in height. His hair was thick and black as Orphan, with the same sun-red highlights.

I'd lost the thread of Maggie's conversation, and I tried to catch up. "—a practice gate," she was saying. "And Scoop will have her accustomed to it in no time, won't you, Scoop?"

I nodded. "I—I'll try."

"I think it's about time we introduced ourselves, don't you, Son? I'm Frederick Fitzsimmons," he said, nodding in a way that made it a bow. "Call me Fitz. Everybody does." He jerked his arm out of his son's grasp. "Quit fussing!" he said gruffly. Then nice again, he said, "And this is my son, Charles Fitzsimmons."

"Call me Charley," he said, grinning and showing two dimples and the greenest eyes I'd ever seen. I wondered if he wore tinted contacts.

"So this is Horsefeathers," said Mr. Fitzsimmons, letting his gaze move from the barn to the pastures, to our horses scattered all over the lawn grazing. "Well," he said slowly, "I think everything looks very comfortable. Don't you, Charley?"

"If I were a horse, I'd think this was a good place to hang out," Charley said.

"You do?" I said. "I mean, it is!" It was amazing. They'd seen Horsefeathers and our horses at their very worst, and they still wanted to stay.

"You won't regret it, Fitz!" Maggie said. "Scoop can work miracles with your horses."

"Well, I hope you're right about that, Maggie," he said. "Actually, we're in need of only one miracle. Jackson, that's Jacksonian's Justice, is our top mount. He's 3, and we plan to retire him at the end of the year for stud fees. Jackson has been running well, top of his form. He just needs a place to stay while we're at the races. It's the filly who needs the miracle."

"Let me go put our horses back in their pastures out of the way," said Maggie, taking Moby's halter in one hand and grabbing Angel's with the other. She headed for the barn, her tutu swishing as she walked. I wondered if she'd bothered explaining her outfit.

That's when it hit me. Jackson was a stallion. I should have known they'd bring a stallion. Where could we keep him away from the mares? He'd be okay in the stall Carla usually put Ham in. But they'd brought three horses. What if they had more than one stallion? There was no way we could keep them separated and out of trouble.

"Mr. Fitzsimmons," I began, trying to think of the best way to ask him if he had other studs in his trailer.

"Call me Fitz, Scoop," he said. "I insist."

The trailer rocked, and stamping hooves pawed at the floor.

"That would be Melancholy Baby," Charley explained. "She's the reason we were so late today. Melly hates the trailer. I thought we'd never get her loaded."

She. Her. At least one horse wasn't a stallion.

Fitz walked to the trailer and looked in through the wind slats. I followed him, anxious to get a peek at the horses. "Easy, Melly," he said. "Melly has the bloodlines of a champion, but she's still a maiden. So's the other one."

"So it's two fillies then?" I asked, relieved.

"Right," Fitz said, walking to the back of the trailer and working the latch. "But a maiden in racing is a horse of either sex who's never won a race."

I felt stupid, but Fitz smiled, as if he didn't think I was an idiot.

"The problem with Melly is she breaks late from the starting gate. Once she gets out of the gate and gets her senses back, she's faster than any horse on the track." He pulled the rod out of the lock and glanced over at me. "That's where I'm hoping you can help us, Scoop. If Melly could get over her problems with the gate, I think she could surprise all of us."

He opened the trailer and let down the loading ramp. "Not that we expect miracles," he said. "I realize a week isn't very long."

I peered into the trailer. Even though I could just see rumps and hind legs sticking out of their green stable blankets, I could tell these were incredible animals. Muscled haunches sat on slender, fine-boned legs that were wrapped in heavy, protective boots.

"Let me get Storm first," Charley said, easing past me and up the ramp to a black mare, or filly more likely, since she didn't look older than 3 or 4 years. She looked to be half a hand shorter than the horse next to her.

Charley unsnapped the lead and got nuzzled as a thank-you. "This beauty is High Wind Hurricane, better known as Storm. And she's mine." She followed her owner down the wooden ramp.

She had on a green face mask, but I could see her eyes through the holes, and she didn't seem a bit nervous.

"She looks like she's a beauty under all that covering," I said.

Maggie joined Charley. "Scoop, you'll have to catch Cheyenne and Misty," she said. She reached inside Storm's mask to scratch her cheek. "Is your Storm a champion too, Charley?"

Before Charley could answer, Fitz said, "Storm? Nah. She's a maiden, but with less promise than Melly. We bring her along as an Also Eligible, in case we have to scratch one of the others. If we need to, we can use her as a Lead Pony to escort one of the Thoroughbreds onto the track."

I wished Jen Zucker could have been there. She reads all the time and is a walking encyclopedia about horses. I'd have to call her and find out what all the racing terms meant. There was so much I didn't know.

"But Storm's ready to Break Maiden, to win her first race," Charley said.

"That'll be the day," Fitz countered.

Orphan nudged me from behind, making me step forward onto the ramp. I put my arm over her neck. "This is Orphan. She actually runs things around here. Right, girl? I think she's telling me your horses have been cooped up in here long enough."

I thought I detected a wave of doubt pass over Fitz's face. But he grinned and stepped back. "I suppose you might as well get to know them. That one's Jackson. He shouldn't give you any trouble."

I told Orphan to stand back, and Maggie stood ready by the tailgate ramp.

"Hey there, Jackson," I murmured, getting around him where he could look me over. His nostrils moved in and out, so I blew gently into them, and he returned the favor. "Buddies already?" I said, trying to find a place on his body that wasn't covered with green blanket. I clipped on his lead and backed him out of the trailer.

"He's gorgeous!" Maggie exclaimed as I passed the bay off to her and went back inside for Melancholy Baby.

"Be careful, Scoop!" Fitz called. "That horse is not herself in the box."

The filly shifted her weight and flattened her ears back when I walked to her head. She was a light chestnut, about Jackson's height. Besides all the stable blankets of the other two horses, poor Melly wore blinders too. When I touched her withers, she trembled.

"It's okay, Melly," I said. Inside I prayed it really would be okay. I could sense Fitz and Charley watching me, no doubt seeing this as some sort of test whether I could handle the job.

God, help me connect with this race horse.

I scratched behind the filly's ears, on her cheek, under her jaw. Nothing. No sign of relaxing. When I stroked her neck, over the neck covering, her ears flew back again. Slowly raising my hand, I tried her withers, touching her shoulder and gradually moving up, increasing pressure to a scratch. As I scratched, I felt her relax and move with my fingers. I'd found her favorite spot.

Melly turned and stared at me front-on, her eyes mostly shrouded by the blinders and face mask. I gazed into her soft, brown eyes, amazed at the clarity and intelligence I saw there. Then something happened, something beyond the connection I sense with almost all horses. As Melly kept her honest gaze on me, I felt a warmth inside, an instant kinship.

The filly must have sensed it too. Her ears flicked up, and her neck stretched across the stall until she could rub against my chest. She let me untie her and back her down the ramp without a problem.

Orphan waited a few paces back. When I looked at my mare, for a minute I almost felt guilty. I'll never love another horse as much as I love Orphan, but I think Orphan sensed my instant bonding with Melly. And she was as confused by it as I was.

4

W ell, I'd say we've made the right choice coming to Horsefeathers!" said Fitz. "Wouldn't you say so, Charley?"

"No kidding," Charley said, falling in behind me with Storm as I walked Melly toward the barn. "I never saw Melly take to anybody like that. Wait 'til Julio sees it." Charley turned back to Maggie, who was leading Jackson behind Storm. "Julio is our trainer. He's really good. Doesn't speak a bit of English, but he sure does speak horse."

"Sounds like Scoop," Maggie said, bringing up the rear with Jackson.

We settled the horses in their stalls, with Jackson in Ham's box stall at one end of the barn, and Melly and Storm neighbors at the other end. When we walked back outside, Fitz was closing the trailer. Cheyenne was rearing to show off to the horses in the paddock, and Misty and Orphan grazed peacefully not a foot apart.

"Well, girls," said Fitz, stepping around to the front of his truck to meet us. "If you don't mind, I'd like to go over a few instructions with you now. Julio and Manny will be out before dawn tomorrow to exercise the horses. They're bringing a practice gate for you to work on with Melly. Charley and I will get us a room out on the highway a few miles north. We'll come back tomorrow and see how you're doing."

"Tomorrow's Sunday, Scoop," Maggie whispered. Louder, she said, "Scoop goes to church in the morning."

Fitz looked surprised. "Well, I don't suppose we'll get around until afternoon anyway." He turned to his son and said sharply, "What are standing around here for, Charley? Get the feed out of the truck."

"Our other partner, Jen Zucker, makes our feed with her own secret formula she's researched," Maggie said. "Everybody who uses it claims it's the best they've ever put their horses on."

"I'm sure it is," Fitz said. "But we can't risk the change. We'll just stick with our own feed for now. Maybe after the racing season."

After the racing season? Was Fitz already looking ahead to a long-term relationship with Horsefeathers Stable?

"Can I help?" I asked, when Charley came out of the truck with a huge bag of feed over his shoulder.

"I got it," he said, grunting between the words.

I led him to our grain room, where we keep the horses' feed in airtight bins that looked like trash cans. Jen's other ingredients were stored on shelves against one wall. An oatmeal smell lingered over the room.

Charley set down the feed bag. "Wow! This is great."

"I'll empty one of the bins for your feed later," I said.

As we walked out of the barn together, Charley told me how much grain each of the horses received daily. Outside, Maggie was obviously entertaining Fitz, who laughed as he listened to the ballerina. Her arms moved as if she were doing pantomime.

"You really run the stable by yourself?" Charley asked.

"Maggie helps. And two of my other friends, Jen and Carla, help as much as they can," I said.

"Still, it's got to be a lot of work," he said. "At the Farms, we have grooms and trainers and even jockeys to help us." He glanced at me. I didn't look up, but I could feel it. "Still, this is the part I love, being around the horses."

"Don't you love horse racing?" I asked. "I thought it was in your veins or something."

"It's in Dad's veins all right. I guess it's in mine too." He smiled, and I was sure he was blushing. "Dad loves racing, and I mostly love horses. That's the difference. But I'd still give just about anything to see Storm win. Nobody would be more surprised than my dad."

Maggie and Fitz stopped talking when we walked up. "Charley," Fitz said, "did I hear you going on about having Storm win a race?" He sighed and shook his head. "That boy's got a lot to learn about racing."

"So do I," I said. "Thanks for giving me the chance to learn it."

Fitz climbed into the truck. "Charley, you stay here and get the horses settled in. I'll go check us into the motel and come back for you." He rolled down his window and motioned me over. "Remember what I said about keeping the horses stalled. I don't want them wasting their energy out in the pasture running for nothing."

It was an instruction he'd given me twice over the phone the first time he'd called. I hated the idea of horses being cooped up at Horsefeathers Stable. "What about letting them out to graze or to get fresh air for an hour after supper? Or I could turn them loose in the paddock? I'd keep an eye on them the whole time and wouldn't let them gallop. And I wouldn't let Jackson out with the fillies."

Fitz shook his head. "No, Scoop. I mean it."

The image of Melly's big, sad eyes ran through my mind. "What if I just led them around—?"

"Scoop," Fitz said firmly, "why do you think

Thoroughbred race horses run so hard on the track when they get the chance?"

"I always thought they were scared or got caught up in the excitement," I said. I knew it wasn't natural for a horse, any horse, to run full out for longer than several yards, and only then if chased. "Why do they do it?" I asked.

"Well, they do get caught up in the emotion of the event. Excitement and fear are part of the reason they run on the track," Fitz admitted. "But another part is that they live the rest of their lives in box stalls. Since they're used to confinement, they're ready to take advantage of the chance to run it out. So keep them in the stalls."

He glanced over at Misty and Orphan and Cheyenne, who were still loose, grazing in front of the barn, enjoying their freedom. "I can't have them getting out. Understood?"

"Understood," I said.

We watched the trailer bounce down the lane as Fitz drove off by himself.

"I need to get home and change my clothes," Maggie said. "Can you get the horses back to the pasture without me?"

"I'll help," Charley offered.

"All right then," Maggie said, with a wink to me and a pirouette to the world. "Have fun!"

"What can I do?" Charley asked after Maggie had left.

"I better get Cheyenne first," I said.

"The Paint out there? She's really pretty," he said.

"She belongs to a friend of mine, Jen Zucker. You'll have to meet Jen. She knows a lot about horses, and everything else actually." I was halfway to Cheyenne, with Charley right behind me. "Would you mind waiting here?" I asked. "This Paint has a mind of her own."

As I'd done dozens of times before, I play-acted with Cheyenne. As soon as she noticed me, she arched her neck and raised her tail, ready to prance or bolt away if I took another step.

I spread my arms out at my sides. "Don't you come over here!" I called, holding my ground. Cheyenne nickered softly and licked her lips. "No you don't!" I called, when she took a step in my direction. It only took a minute more, and she almost begged permission to come to me. Finally, I dropped my arms and called her. She trotted right to me and let me lead her by her halter through the barn and out to pasture.

"On TV, I saw a guy do something like that with wild Mustangs," Charley said. "That was amazing. Now what?"

I whistled to Orphan, and she stopped grazing, nickered back, and walked up to me. Misty followed when I led Orphan to the paddock. Charley trailed behind and closed the stall door after us.

"Cute colt," he said, walking up to Misty

and petting his neck. When Misty turned his head, Charley took hold of the halter. "No you don't, fella. "Don't bite me."

I joined them. "I'll have to have another talk with my little brother about sugar cubes." We both stroked the colt in silence for a minute.

"My dad knows just about everybody in the racing world," Charley said. "Horsefeathers will probably become famous after County Downs." He laughed softly. "Especially after Storm breaks the track record."

Misty's halter felt too tight. I unbuckled the strap to loosen it, but something didn't feel quite right. The leather was too stiff.

"Let me hold him," Charley said, putting his arms around Misty's neck and holding the halter in place while I worked the strap into the buckle. "What's the *D* for?" Charley asked.

"Huh?"

"The D—on your halter?"

I looked where Charley was pointing. High on the side strap was a little, silver D. My stomach rolled over. *D?* Misty's halter didn't have a silver D on it.

"I thought you said the foal's name was Misty," Charley said.

"Uh huh," I answered. *D*, as in Dalton? It had to be. This halter wasn't Misty's. Misty's was worn at the edges and needed a good saddle soaping. This halter looked almost new—and it had a silver D. This halter belonged to Dalton Stables. My brother must have taken it from the Daltons!

"Scoop?" Charley asked, sounding concerned. "Are you okay?"

I tried to nod, but my muscles had turned to steel. *Thanks a lot, B.C.! Stolen property? What's that going to do for our reputation?*

From the front of the barn a horn beeped twice. "Charley! Come on! Time to go!" I hadn't even heard Fitz drive up.

"I have to leave," Charley said, scurrying out of the paddock. "See you tomorrow, Scoop!"

The second they were out of sight, I raced to the tack box. There on top of the tack sat two tan brushes and a metal comb. The brushes weren't white, and they were probably twice as expensive as the lost ones. I threw the brushes into an empty feed bag. Then I ran to Misty, took off the halter and threw it in with the brushes.

I whistled for Orphan, hooked a lead rope to her halter, and jumped on her broad back. The silver D was branded into my brain. I could see it wherever I looked. "B.C.," I muttered through clenched teeth. "You've really done it this time!"

5

Orphan and I cantered down Horsefeathers Lane. The sun was caught between two clouds and sent beams that reached the horizon. The wind picked up, blowing swirls of dust across the lane and forcing me to squint. I leaned forward and urged Orphan into a gallop. Her mane tickled my cheek as I hovered over her neck.

But I didn't hear the horse music, the real soul music of riding, when God and nature and Orphan and I race together in bursts of joy. I didn't hear a note. All I heard were Charley's words: "What's the *D* for?"

The D? I should have said. *Why that's for Dalton, the stable my brother steals from.* If Stephen or his dad heard about this, they'd have our heads—and our reputation. They'd spread the word fast, and Fitz and Charley would be too afraid to leave their horses with us.

By the time Orphan and I trotted up our driveway, I was angrier than I'd been at the barn. I jumped off Orphan, unhooked her lead rope, and let her graze in the tall grass, where an old washing machine sat rusted and cockeyed on what was supposed to be our lawn.

Dotty's Chevy was parked crooked—half on the lawn, half in the drive. She'd left the back door on the driver's side open, so I slammed it shut.

"Orphan, stay here!" I commanded, sure that she wouldn't wander off when she could be grazing in the uncut yard. I stomped across the lawn and charged up the steps to our front porch. Before I could holler inside, I heard a plunk on the porch. I looked down and was plunked on top of my head. I covered my head, and felt something sharp and metal bounce off my arm. B.C.'s bottle caps.

"B.C.!" I screamed. "Stop it!"

He answered by raining down more of the old bottle caps. Every day before our dad was killed, he used to bring B.C. home a pocketful of bottle caps from the plant. B.C. has a million of them. Over the years he's used those caps to create a metal sandpile, to play construction with his caps and toy truck, and to build bottle cap cities. He'd learned his letters and numbers with bottle caps. He sorted them by colors and letters, and used little piles of caps to work out math problems. And he used his bottle caps for weapons.

I protected my head with crossed arms as B.C. threw down a big load of caps. "Okay, then," I said, picking up a handful of them. "I'll just keep your bottle caps and throw them away."

"No! You give me back my bottle caps!" B.C. screamed. He kicked ferociously against the roof. "They're mine!"

"Scoop? Is that you?" Dotty came to the front door and peered through the screen. She still had on her Hy-Klas grocery store uniform — black pants and orange over-shirt, with a "Hi! I'm Dottie" nametag on the front. Her short brown hair looked like she'd put in a hard day at the check-out counter. Wiping her hands on her apron, she pushed the screen door open with her shoulder and lumbered out to the porch. "Everything all right, Scoop? I thought I heard shouting."

One look at Dotty, and some of my anger fizzled. I've observed the same phenomenon with horses. One gentle horse in a herd of wild horses can help calm all of them. Maggie calls Dotty peacefully, pleasingly plump. Her arms are thick and soft as bread dough. She's a full two inches shorter than I am, maybe 5'3", but she always seems taller than anyone else in the room.

I nodded to the roof and B.C. "Ask him why I'm so mad."

Dotty looked up to the roof and almost stumbled over a bottle cap. "I reckon it's them bottle caps. You ain't been throwing them caps again, have you, B.C.?"

"It's Scoop's fault!" B.C. yelled. "She was mean to me at the barn, and she yelled at me, and now she says she's going to take all my bottle caps and throw them away!"

"Scoop?" Dotty said softly. "You ain't gone and threatened to take the boy's bottle caps away?"

This wasn't fair! I wasn't supposed to be the one who got blamed. "Dotty! B.C.'s the one who—"

"I reckon we ought to come inside and have us a talk," Dotty said.

"Yeah!" I said. "Get down here, B.C.!"

B.C. didn't budge.

Dotty opened the screen door and started in. Over her shoulder she said in a normal voice, "B.C., come down now."

B.C. jumped from the roof and pushed by me. "Don't touch my bottle caps!" he yelled, as he shoved me to get through the door first.

I followed him inside, where only the kitchen light glowed. The living room smelled old, a cross between rusty metal and rotten bananas. B.C. already had the TV on. He plopped into the vinyl chair and started picking at the strip of gray duct tape on the arm of the chair.

Ignoring B.C., I walked through to the kitchen, where Dotty was in the middle of setting out dinner: salami wrapped in white paper, a loaf of white bread, and two plastic containers of something that was probably the Hy-Klas special of the week. I got out forks and spoons. "Can we talk first, Dotty?" I asked, arranging forks on the left, spoons on the right.

"I reckon this food will keep," she said. The food had probably been keeping for a week at the store. "B.C.!" Dotty called. "Turn off the TV and come sit a spell with Scoop and me."

We sat at the kitchen table together, B.C. scooting his chair closer to Dotty than usual, as if he were afraid of me.

"Before we start, Lord," Dotty said, pulling B.C. onto her lap, even though he was almost a fifth grader, "please make us honest before You Help us always to do the right thing. What's this really about?"

It took me a second to realize the last question was for me instead of God. Dotty's praying voice isn't like you hear on TV. She talks to God in a regular voice, as if He's in the chair next to her.

"I'll tell you!" B.C. screamed, pointing at me. "She said she was going to throw away my bottle caps!"

"Is that true, Scoop?" Dotty asked, her forehead folding into a wave of wrinkles

"Yeah, it's true," I admitted. "But I wouldn't have. You know I wouldn't throw his stupid caps away."

"Do you think you ought to apologize to B.C. for—" Dotty began.

"Dotty! He's the one who should be apologizing to me!"

"Well, maybe if you can get your apology over with first, B.C. can take his turn at sorry," Dotty suggested.

I clenched my teeth so tight I thought my jaws would explode. Taking a deep breath, I let the words out as an exhale: "I'm sorry I said I'd throw your bottle caps away." Actually at that moment I was sorrier that I hadn't gone through with it.

"That was real nice, Scoop," Dotty said. "Wasn't that real nice, B.C.?"

B.C. shrugged.

"Now B.C.," Dotty said, stroking his thick brown hair, smoothing it back out of his eyes. "What do you reckon got Scoop so upset?"

B.C. shrugged, as if he had no idea why I was crazy mad.

"Fine!" I said. "Then I'll tell you why I'm upset."

B.C. shook his head several times. "She's mad at me because I couldn't remember where I put the new brushes."

"Well," Dotty said, patting B.C.'s head against her round shoulder, "I reckon you still got lots to learn about being responsible. You want to tell Scoop you're sorry for misplacing them brushes?"

"That's not the worst of it, Dotty!" I said. "Make him tell you what he did."

B.C. looked at the ceiling. He studied the floor. Then he stared at the clock over the sink. His foot moved in little kicks against the table.

"Tell her, B.C.! Tell her about the halter and the brushes."

He examined his fingernails and didn't answer me.

"What halter is that?" Dotty asked. I shoved the bag with the brushes and halter inside across the table to Dotty. She just left it there and looked at B.C.

I couldn't wait any longer for B.C. to fess up. "We got this new client I told you about, Dotty."

"Them race horse people?" she asked.

"Yeah. And everything was going great until Charley, Mr. Fitzsimmons's son, was petting Misty and saw a big letter D on the halter. A *D*, Dotty!"

"I don't rightly follow, Scoop. "Why was Misty wearing a halter with a *D*?"

"Because my little brother stole the halter from Dalton Stables! And he stole brushes too! I was so embarrassed, Dotty! If Mr. Fitzsimmons finds out what B.C. did, that will be the end of Horsefeathers' reputation."

B.C. studied the nearest spoon and never looked up once.

"B.C., honey," Dotty began, "did you take something that don't belong to you?"

B.C. shrugged, and I got angrier, visualizing Charley and Fitz asking to take their horses back.

"Admit it, B.C.!" I insisted. "You stole those things!"

B.C.'s head jerked up. "I did not steal! I borrowed them because you were so mad at me for losing stuff. Daltons have a million halters and brushes. They don't need all that stuff, and you really do need it, and I couldn't find the new ones at Horsefeathers, so I kept looking in the pasture, and before I knew it I was at Dalton Stables, and nobody was there, and I just saw this stuff lying around and—" His voice grew higher and louder with every word.

"Calm down, B.C.," Dotty said. "We'll make it right. It's gonna be all right, ain't it, Scoop?"

"No, Dotty!" I cried. "It's not going to be all right. What if our new boarders decide we're a bunch of thieves? What if the word gets out that nothing is safe at Horsefeathers?"

"That will all work itself out," Dotty said calmly, rocking with B.C. in her lap like she used to do when he was little. B.C's shoulders shook, as if he were shivering, although it was at least as hot inside as it was out.

"The most important thing right now, I reckon," Dotty said, still rocking my brother, "is to help B.C. make things right with God."

I wanted to argue. Even if B.C. and God got all squared away, that still left me and Horsefeathers in a fix. I'd taken on race horses to give my stable a better reputation. Stealing wasn't going to help.

"The Lord knows you didn't think you was stealing," Dotty said. "But taking something what ain't yours, that *is* stealing. You understand, B.C.?"

"I was going to give them back," B.C. said, sniffing between words. His whole body slumped, as if his bones had evaporated on him.

"I know you was, B.C.," Dotty said. "But we gotta make amends. I reckon you ought to get them things back to the Daltons and tell them you're right sorry."

"Wait a minute!" I protested. "You mean he has to tell them he's the thief?"

"I'm not a thief!" B.C. cried.

"Of course you ain't, B.C.," Dotty said. "That's why you're going to get right over to them Daltons and tell them how you done took without asking and say your sorries."

"He can't do that, Dotty!" I insisted. "Then they'll be suspicious of Horsefeathers for sure! And they're bound to tell everybody. You know they will! What about our reputation?"

Dotty wasn't listening. I knew she was probably praying in her head, discussing all this with

God instead of with me. "The most important thing here is that B.C. does what God wants him to do. The only reputation that figures is ours with our Maker. Lord, thank You for bringing this here to light. Thank You that You forgive us when we done wrong. You'll have to go with B.C."

I was praying that Dotty was still talking to God. "Go with him? Not me, Dotty. You can't mean you want me to go with him to the Daltons!"

"I reckon that's the right thing to do. You got Orphan out there. You could ride over in no time flat. We'll eat supper when you get home."

There's no use arguing with Dotty once she's sure she knows what God wants, but I tried anyway. Minutes later, after I'd run out of arguments, I whistled for Orphan. Orphan sidled up to the front porch, and I stepped onto her back. Dotty handed me the bag of stolen goods and helped B.C. mount up behind me.

"Hold on," I said, as Orphan took off at a trot and B.C. bounced. "Let's get this over with."

Orphan broke into a gentle lope, which we kept most of the way to Dalton Stables. At the edge of Dalton's fences, I pulled Orphan up. I hardly recognized the place. People and horses moved around like ants on an ant hill. At least three horses pranced around the outside arena, while three more were being led in front of the stable.

"Wow!" B.C. said.

"No kidding," I muttered.

Dalton Stables is usually a pretty busy place, with a couple of full-time grooms and more horses than you can count on two sets of toes. But that was nothing compared to this. Four more Thoroughbreds were hooked to a hot walker, which kept them circling at a walk. I recognized Mr. Langhorne and his trailer. Lawrence stood with Ursula and Stephen next to the barn.

I urged Orphan closer and tried to find Ralph Dalton, Stephen's father. The best way to do this with the least amount of publicity would be to get Ralph Dalton off by himself. I spotted him as he came out from behind the black trailer.

"You did the stealing, B.C.," I said. "You do the talking."

I waved to Mr. Dalton, but he didn't seem to see me. Instead, he strolled over to the barn, by Ursula. Great! Might as well let the whole world in on it.

"Scoop?" Stephen Dalton called. "What are you doing here?"

Ursula, Lawrence, and Stephen's dad turned to look. With all four staring me, I couldn't get any words to come out. "I—that is—B.C.—"

"You're the girl from Horsefeathers!" Lawrence shouted, chuckling, confirming my lousy first impression of the guy.

"You know her?" Stephen asked, as if he couldn't imagine such a thing.

"Not really," Lawrence said.

Ursula smoothed back her bleached blonde hair. "My father does not like the public to watch workouts before racing events."

"We're not here to watch," I said, my voice cracking. I reached back and squeezed B.C.'s thigh. "Now, B.C.," I whispered.

"Ursula's right, Scoop," said Ralph Dalton. "I'm afraid we'll have to ask you to leave."

I held out the brown bag of stolen property and elbowed my brother. "B.C. did something he's sorry for. Right, B.C.?"

I felt him nod. "Sorry," he muttered.

"He didn't really mean to keep that stuff," I explained. "He lost my brushes and Misty's halter, and I yelled at him; so he kind of borrowed these. But he should have asked." It felt weird to find myself defending B.C., when a few minutes earlier I'd been ready to throw him in jail myself.

"I don't understand," said Mr. Dalton. "What does all this have to do with—"

"Here!" I said, tossing down the brown bag. "We're sorry. It won't happen again."

Ralph Dalton opened the bag as if I might have stuffed it with tarantulas. He pulled out the halter with the letter D on it. "Why, this is one of ours!" he exclaimed, as amazed as if he'd just pulled a rabbit out of a hat.

"Let me see that," Stephen said, taking the halter from his dad. "That's ours all right. Brother! I knew we had tack thieves around here. I just didn't know they lived next door." He glared up at me. "So where's the other stolen stuff?"

W hat did you say?" I asked, hoping I'd heard him wrong, praying I'd heard him wrong.

"I said," Stephen repeated, waving a brush in the air as if he were a prosecutor with evidence that would send us to prison for life, "where is the rest of our tack?"

I twisted around to see B.C.'s face. His eyes were big and watery.

"I didn't take anything else," he whispered.

"Are you totally sure, B.C.?" I asked.

"Honest! Only the two brushes, one comb, and the halter. That's all, Scoop! You have to believe me. I didn't steal anything else."

Turning back to the accusers, I said, "There must be some mistake."

"The mistake is you!" Stephen shouted. "I should have figured it was a Coop who was stealing from us."

I felt like I'd been kicked in the stomach. I wanted to pivot Orphan and gallop away as fast as I could. Ursula and her brother stood back, watching as if they were afraid I was armed and dangerous.

A man led a sorrel stallion out of the barn. The horse had a red stable blanket that covered his head, neck, and body. Two more men rode horses out from the paddock. The riders didn't touch their English racing saddles, as they supported themselves on short, metal stirrups. They all gave B.C. and me sideways glances that made me want to dig a hole and crawl into it.

"We haven't been stealing," I explained. "B.C. meant to bring these things back. This is all he took."

Ralph Dalton put the stolen items back in the bag. "We've had it up to here with tack thieves." He gestured with his right hand that he'd had it up to his forehead.

Lawrence strolled up to Ralph Dalton. "We have the same problem upstate," he said. "There's a lot of money in stealing saddles and bridles, more than people think."

Great! Now I'm going to be accused of stealing from all over the state? "Look," I said. "We apologize. It won't happen again."

"It better not, Scoop," Stephen said.

"Well," said his father, "this isn't a new problem for us. I don't think we're missing more than usual. You go on home. And it would be best if you stayed off Dalton land until after the County Downs races. I promised the Langhorne's top security." He headed to the barn with Lawrence and Ursula on his heels.

"Thank you," I called after him. But I didn't feel thankful. I felt raw. I felt branded. I wondered if they believed me. I wondered if I believed B.C. He'd lied to me once about stealing.

"You surprise me, B.C.," Stephen said, as I turned Orphan back toward Horsefeathers. "I didn't think you had it in you. But I should have known, I suppose. Stealing must run in the family."

I squeezed my thighs and gave Orphan the signal to canter. Stephen had to back-pedal to get out of our way. I felt B.C.'s arms around my waist and his head on my back as we rode through the pastures. I wished I'd never yelled at him about the brushes in the first place.

It wasn't until we were back at Horsefeathers and I'd finished cooling off Orphan and doing evening chores that B.C. spoke. "Scoop?" he said, as I filled the last hay net in Jackson's stall. "What did Stephen mean about stealing running in our family?"

I'd been hoping against hope he wouldn't ask. "Oh, I don't know, B.C.," I said, not looking at him. "You know Stephen."

B.C. wouldn't let it go. "But he said stealing ran in our family, and he should have known it was a Coop who was stealing. Did our folks steal?"

I turned and studied my little brother. He looked so helpless and sad, his cheeks muddy from a mix of dirt and tears. Shutting in Jackson, I joined B.C. in the stallway and made him sit with me on a bale of hay. It was dark outside, and the only light in the barn came from an overhead bulb that wrapped B.C. in shadows.

"You listen to me, B.C.," I said, choking back tears that pushed in my throat. "Our parents were good people. They were poor and maybe not as educated or as fancy as the Daltons, but they were good people who never would have stolen anything. Got it?"

B.C. shifted on the bale. "Then why did Stephen say that?"

I took a deep breath. I'd never wanted B.C. to find out, but he was going to sooner or later. I might as well be the one to tell him. "Stephen was talking about me."

Even in the dark I could see his confused, contorted face. "You? You never stole nothing! Stephen's a liar!"

"You don't know how much I wish it was just a lie." I had to pause and collect the words, line them up so they'd come out in order. "I was 10—"

"Like me?" B.C. interrupted.

"Like you. Mom and Dad had been dead for about three years. But for some reason, it started to feel like they'd just died again."

"I feel like that sometimes," B.C. said softly. "And sometimes it feels like it was my fault."

"B.C.!" I said. "No way was—"

"It's okay, Scoop," he said, sounding like the older brother instead of the runt. "I know it wasn't my fault. But it still feels like it sometimes. Did you feel like that when you were my age?"

"I don't know what I felt, B.C.," I said. This was a memory I'd worked hard at erasing. Now it came flooding back as if I were watching myself in a movie. "I kind of remember not feeling anything—not happy or sad or scared—just numb."

In the dark, B.C. reached over and took my hand in his small hand.

"Then one day when I was waiting on Dotty at the Hy-Klas, I was staring at the rows and rows of gum—red packs and pink and green and blue, some of them in the wrong row. And I just reached up and took a green pack and shoved it in my pocket. It was weird—like I was getting even with somebody, getting away with something, I guess."

Something scratched at my leg. Then Dogless Cat, our barn cat, sprang up and curled himself in my lap, easing into a loud, steady purr. Above us, barn swallows swooped to the loft rafters. One of the horses sneezed. B.C. squeezed my hand.

"The next day I returned the gum. I hadn't

taken it out of my pocket. But when I put it back and straightened the rows, I took two more packs, a pink and a blue. All day I remember sticking my hand in my pocket and feeling the packs of gum, as if they were the only things real in my life, the only part of my life I had any control over or any say in.

"I went on like that, taking gum and putting it back, for a couple of days I think. Then one day, when I was putting back the gum and straightening the rows better than they'd been, Mr. Ford nabbed me."

"Did you run?" B.C. asked.

"I couldn't have run if I'd wanted to, B.C.," I said, feeling Mr. Ford's grip on my collar again.

"Were you scared? What did they do to you? Did Dotty find out?"

"I don't remember being scared, which is pretty weird looking back on it now."

"I would have been scared," B.C. said.

"I think I just didn't care about anything that summer—until Mr. Ford called Dotty over and told her he'd caught me stealing."

"Did you tell her you weren't stealing? Did you tell her you were just putting the gum back? That you didn't even chew any of it?"

B.C. sounded agitated, desperate. I hoped I hadn't made a mistake by telling him. But now that I'd started, I had to finish. "I didn't try to lie my way out of it—not because I was a good kid, but because I was just too tired."

"What did Dotty do?" B.C. asked.

A picture flashed through my mind—Dotty's puzzled face when Mr. Ford called her away from the cash register to inform her that her niece was a thief. Sorrow welled up in her eyes, an agony I'd never seen in her.

"What did she do?" B.C. asked louder.

"I'll tell you what she did, B.C.," I answered. "Dotty calmly took off her apron and said very politely, 'Mr. Ford, me and Scoop need to talk. I'll take my break now.'"

"She didn't yell at you or cry or anything?" B.C. asked.

The barn had grown darker, and the overhead light bulb blinked. Something swooped over our heads, probably a bat.

"Nope," I said. "Dotty didn't yell. Instead, she took me to the roof of the Hy-Klas and sat me down beside her."

"Dotty? Our Dotty climbed to the roof?" B.C. asked, amazed.

"Yep. And she told me about how Christ died to pay for the things we do wrong, including stealing. And that He raised from the dead to prove it. And we prayed for forgiveness right there on the roof, even when it started to rain."

I was quiet for a minute, picturing the whole scene—Dotty's orange uniform soaked clear through, drops of water on her thick glasses, one bare foot because she'd lost the shoe on the climb to the roof. "I never stole again, B.C." Dotty called it repentance, deciding not to do wrong again because Christ went through so much so we could experience God's forgiveness. "I never will."

In the dark, B.C.'s little voice pierced like a pinprick. "Me neither."

7

Sunday in church it was impossible to keep my mind on the sermon. None of the Daltons showed. They were probably too caught up with training the race horses and fussing over Ursula's family.

After the service, I filled Travis and Jen Zucker in on our new clients. We stood in the front of the sanctuary, exchanging information and ideas while the church emptied.

"I don't get it," Travis said. "How do they expect you to get this Melancholy horse trained to the starting gate by Friday?" His blond hair looked blonder from the sun and his eyes bluer than sky. If he'd been born a horse, he would have made a great Palomino stallion. He's 17, and Maggie 37 had had a crush on him since fifth grade. Who could blame her?

"Travis is right, Scoop," Jen said. She turned her head and sneezed. "They should have given you more time."

Jen looked thinner than usual. She usually reminded me of the Kathiawari horse found on the coast of India. They're more narrowly built than Arabians and have the reputation of being highly intelligent. Plus, the Kathiawari is courageous, like Jen, who's battling a serious kidney disease. I wanted to ask her how she was doing, but she hates that. So I pretended I didn't see the pain on her face when she sneezed.

"I've been reading up on race horses," Jen said, after a mild coughing fit. "Maybe Travis and I can stop by Horsefeathers later."

"That would be great!" I said. I caught Travis's signal. He was standing behind his sister, shaking his head no at me. I knew he meant it wouldn't be good for Jen to get out to the barn today.

"But you know," I said, "on second thought, tomorrow would work a lot better. The horses are just settling in today. And the trainer wants to work all of the horses himself. I won't even get to exercise any of them until tomorrow. And the practice gate won't be up before then either. Besides—"

"I get it," Jen said, flashing a knowing look to Travis, then to me. "Okay. We'll be out tomorrow."

I hurried home after church, changed clothes, and took a sandwich to eat on the way to Horsefeathers. B.C. insisted on tagging along, and Dotty backed him up. Before the barn came into sight, unfamiliar sounds reached us—a cranking noise of iron on iron, a clang, like the slamming of a gate, and foreign whinnies and nickers.

Two men were leading Melly and Jackson around the paddock. From the looks of the horses' wet, foamy bodies, they had already had their exercise. One of the men shouted in Spanish to the other one, and they turned back toward the barn.

"What are they doing?" B.C. asked. "Where's Misty?"

As if the colt had heard B.C., Misty let out a long whinny. B.C. and I ran to the south pasture to greet our horses. Orphan stood a few yards back from the paddock, surveying the new horses and the strange activity on her turf. I stroked her white blaze, and she nuzzled my neck.

"Scoop!" Charley rode up on Storm. He wore a brown helmet, tan stretch pants, or jodhpurs, and a long-sleeved, green shirt. If he hadn't been so tall, he'd have looked like a jockey. He pulled Storm up next to the fence. The mare nickered to Orphan, and Orphan answered her.

"Hey, Charley," I said, rubbing Storm's sweaty head. She jerked and chomped the bit. "This is my little brother, B.C."

But B.C. stayed hidden behind me, as if that made him invisible.

"Glad to meet you, B.C. I'll bet you're a big

help to your sister around here." Charley leaned down and adjusted his leather boot in the silver stirrup.

"Don't your legs get sore bent in two like that?" I asked.

"You get used to it," he said, standing in the stirrups, which made him tower over his mount.

B.C. stayed with Misty while Charley introduced me to Julio and Manny, the trainers. I helped him scrape sweat off Storm. "Storm's a beautiful horse," I said, as we rubbed her down.

"She can be a champion too," Charley said, "in spite of what Dad says. I'm really thinking County Downs could be the place where Storm shows them what she's made of."

I had a feeling he was talking about his dad ... and himself. "What race is Storm entered in?" I asked.

"She's signed on as Eligible. So she could take Melly's or Jackson's place if they don't run well. I keep trying to get Dad to enter her straight out, but he says we need a good backup horse."

When we were returning Storm to her stall, Charley said, "I hear you had words over at Dalton Stables."

My heart turned stone cold. How could word have gotten around so fast? "But—" I sputtered, unable to answer him. "B.C. didn't mean anything by it. I'd yelled at him for losing our brushes, and he——"

"Don't worry," Charley said. "Dad didn't buy a word of it. He figured the Langhornes must be up to something."

"You know the Langhornes?" I asked.

"The racing world's not that big, Scoop." Charley unsnapped Storm's lead rope and left her in her stall. "We've competed against them for years. This is really the first summer we've had the favorite—Jackson. I don't think they know how to handle that. Jackson beat their lead filly, Langhorne's Lucky Lady, twice this year already. He'll be the favorite going into County Downs."

It made me mad to think of the Langhornes gossiping about B.C. and me behind our backs. Ursula, Stephen, and Lawrence hadn't wasted any time running to our new boarders. "Thanks for trusting us, Charley," I said.

B.C. kept to himself the rest of the afternoon and then disappeared. Charley and I watched the trainers work Melly and Jackson. It was late afternoon by the time Julio and Manny finished. We helped them set up a metal contraption that looked like three stalls of an official starting gate. The stalls were cramped, and I could understand why Melly hated this part of racing. Beginning Monday morning, it would be my job to get her more "gate-friendly."

After everyone had left Horsefeathers, I

slipped a hackamore on Orphan and took off for some real riding. We cantered through the pasture, sailed over the creek, thundered up the hill and into the woods, horse music singing all around me as dusk fell.

After cooling off Orphan and graining the other horses, I checked in on Melly. She was pacing in her little box stall, back and forth, back and forth. "Hey, Melly," I called in a low voice to soothe her.

She strode quickly toward me, then turned again to keep up her pacing. The poor horse looked so miserable I could hardly stand it. I wasn't officially supposed to start Melly's gate work until Monday, but by then people would be back. I liked it much better with just horses—and Dogless, who lay in Melly's feed trough watching every step the filly made.

"What's wrong, Melly?" I asked, cautiously stepping into the stall with her. She was so nervous, I saw her shoulder muscle twitch. *Lord,* I prayed, reminding myself to talk to God on the spot, the way Dotty always does. *Please settle Melly down. Show me how to help her.*

"Why are you so afraid?" I asked the filly. I wondered if someone had abused her along the way. Raising my arms over my head, I took a step toward her. She didn't flinch. Nobody had been whipping her, or she would have been frightened of quick arm movements.

I moved in next to her and felt the heat of her body. When I lifted my knee and leg to her belly, she didn't stiffen or grunt, as she would have done if she feared a kick or spur. I stepped back and swung the lead rope over my head. An abused horse, one that's been whipped, will react wildly to the overhead motion. Melly looked at me like I was crazy, but she wasn't afraid.

"Good," I told her, stroking her long, firm neck. "Nobody hurt you, did they, Melly?"

She craned her neck around and locked me with that intense stare of hers. It made me want to help her more than ever.

"Why do you hate the starting gate?" I asked her. Through the barn window, I could glimpse part of the iron monster out in the paddock. It cast long shadows onto the field. The gate stalls were so small, I wouldn't have liked being in there either. I remembered what Charley and Fitz said about Melly not liking to load. I thought about how frightened she'd seemed when I first saw her standing still in the trailer, how anxious she was to break out of there.

And I got an idea. I snapped the lead rope onto Melly's halter and led her closer to the wall of her stall. "Come on, Melly," I coaxed. She let me lead her within inches of the wall. With the rope in my left hand, I placed the flat of my right hand against her free side. Pressing gently, then more firmly, I acted as if I wanted to hold her against the wall.

Immediately, she kicked straight out, then lunged forward, nearly pulling me off my feet. I pulled my hand away. "Easy, Melly," I said. "Easy, Girl."

A thrill ran through me as I realized what was wrong with her. "Melancholy Baby," I said, hugging her around her neck, "you've got claustrophobia!"

8

W hat's clobber-phobia?" B.C. asked as I gulped down a bowl of Tastee-O's, sifting out the weird clumps at the bottom of the bowl.

"Claustrophobia, B.C.," I corrected. "It means you hate to be in small places."

"Like Tommy Zucker when he wouldn't come in my bedroom because he said it was too small?" B.C. asked.

"No, that was just rude," I said. Tommy isn't a bad kid, but he is just too much kid for my brother. Once he had B.C. convinced he was pregnant because he had on a green shirt. Another time Tommy made B.C. sell him his lunch money for a penny every day for a week.

Dotty, already dressed for work, poured water from the tea kettle into the brown grains of instant coffee sitting in her chipped, white coffee cup. "Ain't that like when somebody can't stand to be locked in a closet or—"

"I got that closet-phobia thing!" B.C. exclaimed. "I know I couldn't stand it if somebody went and locked me in the closet! And nobody would be around to get me out. And it would get darker and darker, and there would be like these rats and things in the closet with me. Is it like a disease? Will I get worse and worse until I fade away and then they put me in a wooden box, a coffin like Grandad had, and then put me in the ground and—?"

"Benjamin Coop," Dotty said firmly. "You stop that now, you hear? Lord, help us be thankful for what we got and not worry about things we don't got. Finish your Tastee-O's. Your cartoons will be on in a minute. "

The last part was for B.C., who hadn't touched his cereal and who loves all things animated.

"I have to go," I said, dumping my bowl and spoon into the already-full sink. The faucet was leaking again. Big drops of water dripped and plunked into the chipped, white sink. Dotty had stuck a Band-Aid over the worst of the chips, but it was coming loose. "Dotty, when are you going to get that leaky faucet fixed?"

"I reckon the day after we get the leaky roof repaired," she said, gulping her coffee and dumping it into the sink pile. "You be careful today with them race horses. Can't say as I trust them just yet. It still don't rest easy with me that we got horses some folks bet their life savings on."

"You have to meet Melly, Dotty. Melancholy

Baby is her racing name. She's such a sweetheart—a chestnut with grace and charm and a white blaze that covers her whole muzzle. I know I'm going to be sad when she leaves. There's just something about her, the way she stares at me."

"Like God staring out from one of His creations?" Dotty suggested.

"Wow! I never thought of it like that, but yeah. It does feel that way." It caught me off guard that Dotty knew what I was feeling about a horse. Dotty doesn't know much about horses, but she knows a lot about God, so maybe that was it.

"I reckon God's everywhere, even at the races," Dotty said. "I gotta git to the Hy-Klas. Want a ride?"

~~~~~~~~~~~~~~~~~~~~~~~~~~~~~~

Horsefeathers was alive and bustling already, even though it was before seven. Jackson and Melly were jogging around the paddock, with Fitz standing in the center barking orders at the riders in half-Spanish, half-English. I leaned over the paddock fence next to Charley.

"Morning," I said. "How come you and Storm aren't out there? Or have you already finished? You guys sure know how to get an early start."

Charley grinned, but he didn't look happy. "I'll work Storm when the others are done—

76

Dad's training instruction. He still thinks of my horse as a pony lead. Storm is only 4, but he thinks of her as over-the-hill."

"Storm is only 4?" Cheyenne was our youngest, not counting Misty, and she was 6. "That white mare, Maggie's horse Moby—" I pointed to Moby on the far side of the paddock where she, Orphan, and Misty had a ringside seat. "She's 24 years old."

Charley shook his head. "Not many race horses get to be that old. If they do, they sure don't look that good."

"No puedo el bit, Manny!" yelled Mr. Fitzsimmons.

Misty whinnied, and I wanted to run over and greet her and Orphan. Normally, Orphan would have raced across the paddock to say her morning hello. Today I'd have to walk around the training session to get to Orphan. But Charley seemed so down that I didn't think I should leave him yet. "Will you get to race Storm at County Downs?" I asked.

Charley shrugged. "If I don't, I probably won't get another chance. Dad's right. Four years is old in the race horse business. Melly's 4, and Jackson's 3. You know that all race horses claim January 1 as their birthday, don't you?"

I nodded. I only knew because it was one of the facts Jen had given me over the phone the night before. Most of her information had been negative—like the fact that sometimes race horses' hearts get so big from over-exertion that they burst.

"Racing is really hard on horses. Isn't it, Charley?" I asked, remembering some of the other dangers Jen had explained.

"Yeah," Charley admitted, "I know. But if Storm could stand in the Winner's Circle just one time—one time is all I ask—then I'd put her out to pasture. And we could all live happily ever after."

I changed the subject. "How's the paddock arena working out for training? I know it's way shorter than a race track."

"Julio told Dad it's okay because they don't want to run the horses down. They'll jog them today, do a light gallop. Tomorrow we'll breeze them once or twice."

I wanted to ask him what breezing was, but I already felt too stupid about racing.

Charley must have seen that I didn't understand. "Breezing is running faster than a gallop. Short bursts of speed, that's how the trainer likes to run the horses before a race."

We watched Melly and Jackson trot around the ring for a half hour. Jackson looked like a bomb waiting to explode. His rider had to hold him back the whole way. Melly pranced and chomped at the bit, graceful in every gait. Whenever she passed by us, I got the feeling she was trying to communicate something to me.

Julio and Manny were cooling off the horses when Travis's white beater pickup pulled up the lane. Travis, Jen, and Maggie got out. "Hey, Scoop! Charley!" called Maggie. With her green stretch pants and long, green shirt, Maggie 37 Green fit right in with the Fitzsimmons Stable colors.

Travis introduced himself and his sister to Charley and shook hands. "How's Horsefeathers working out for you?" he asked. Travis could make a turkey feel at ease on Thanksgiving.

"Dad says we've got all we need here—which is pretty amazing. He's a tough one to please," Charley said.

"Well that's great, y'all!" Maggie said, pulling out her Southern belle accent. "I would dearly love to see a race close up and personal."

"You should come and watch us race at the Downs on Friday," Charley said. "I'll get back passes for all of you. Melly and Jackson are in the same race this week. Next week is the claim's stake. I'm not sure who Dad will run there. Depending how those go, the final race is early the following week."

"Charley!" bellowed his father. "Are you working Storm this morning or not?"

"Gotta go." Charley ran into the barn, and we trailed in after him.

"It's weird seeing Horsefeathers like this,

isn't it?" Maggie asked.

"If this works out for Fitzsimmons Stable though, just think of what this could mean for our reputation," Jen said. "We wouldn't have to worry about paying bills, and we could do some repairs too."

"So," Travis said, walking close enough beside me that I had trouble concentrating on anything else, "are you going to gamble now that you have this inside information?"

"Travis!" Jen said. "I am shocked, big brother." Every time I see Jen and Travis together, or with any of the nine Zucker kids, I feel a pang and wonder what it would be like to be part of a family like that. Mr. and Mrs. Zucker would do anything for their kids, even buy them a horse like Cheyenne, who probably wasn't the best family horse but was the one they wanted.

"I wonder if we could make money at the track," Maggie said.

"Maggie!" Jen scolded. We walked through the stall. Manny was scraping sweat from Jackson, and Julio was still leading Melly around to cool her off.

"Which horse would you bet on, Scoop, if you were a betting man?" Maggie asked.

"Melancholy Baby all the way, even if I lost," I said.

We watched Charley run Storm through her paces. He let her run fast on the straightaway a couple of times and was called down by Fitz. After a little while, Travis said he and Jen had to leave. I knew Travis was taking Jen to the clinic for dialysis, a long process where doctors clean her blood. Jen didn't like to talk about it, so she just said bye like she was going out to lunch.

Maggie stayed to help me work with Melly. We waited until the trainers left and Charley finished with Storm. Then Maggie and I walked out to the pasture and examined the practice gate.

"This is horrible!" Maggie exclaimed, touching the rust-colored contraption. She jerked her finger back as if the gate were hot. "No wonder Melly hates it. I wouldn't make Moby go in there. Look how small the sections are. Three horses are supposed to fit in here and get a good start?"

My stomach felt queasy as I entered the middle stall and tried to imagine what Melly felt like boxed in on both sides. "Close the gate, Maggie," I said.

Maggie looked around and finally discovered how to close the front. A metal door slid down with a clash and closed me in, but the back was still open. Then she found that lever and slammed down the back gate. I jumped, and felt my heart skip.

"Hey, not bad!" Charley called, crossing the pasture to us. "I'm putting my money on Scoop to win!"

He opened the gates again. "What do you think?"

"I think I get why Melly is so frightened," I said. I wanted to tell him my theory about claustrophobia, but I was afraid I'd sound too stupid. What if I were wrong, and horses were never really claustrophobic?

"Well," Charley teased, "you ready to try this with a real horse yet?"

"Not quite yet," I said. "Probably not until tomorrow."

"Scoop!" Maggie protested dramatically. "The race is Friday! How can you wait a day?"

"It won't work unless Melly trusts me," I said, hoping I knew what I was talking about. "Do you mind if I get used to Melly first? Would anybody care if I rode her a little bit?"

"The saddles are drying out and getting waxed," Charley said.

"Scoop doesn't believe in saddles," Maggie explained. "Didn't you know that?"

"I don't think Melly's ever been ridden bareback. She's a tall fall if she gets a mind to throw you," Charley said.

"I know," I said.

Charley scratched his head. "If Dad were out here, I don't think he'd like it." He hesitated. "Okay, but you have to wear a jockey's hat just in case."

"Deal."

Melly had some of the best ground manners of any horse I'd ever worked on the lunge line. She walked and trotted on command as I stood in the middle of her circle and watched how gracefully she moved. She wanted to please me.

After 10 minutes on the lunge line, I unhooked her lead and held on to her halter.

"Scoop!" Charley called, from where he and Maggie sat on the fence watching every move. "You can't turn her loose. Dad would kill me!"

"She won't run," I said, sounding surer than I was. *Lord, give me wisdom ... and Melly too,* I prayed. When I let go of her halter, Melly didn't bolt away. I turned my back on her and walked toward Maggie and Charley. The filly followed me, so close I felt her hot horse breath on the back of my neck. I turned and walked over to Orphan. Melly turned and came after me. She followed me all around the paddock, and I knew I had her trust.

"Now I'm ready to ride," I said.

Charley bridled Melly with the broken bit she was used to. "Be careful, Scoop," he said, cupping his hands to give me a leg up. Maggie held the reins. It was a moving-target mount, with me flopped undignified over the filly's back while she sidestepped. Finally I got my leg over.

Orphan is just over 15 and a half hands, and Carla's horse Ham is about 17. Melly had to be 17.3 or better. The ground looked a long way down. "Easy, Melly," I murmured, stroking her neck until I felt her quit her twitching. "Let's just have a nice ride. You're going to enjoy this, whether you like it or not."

Maggie was still holding the reins. "She's so big, Scoop!"

"I noticed," I said. "Open the paddock. I want to ride in the pasture."

"I don't know," Charley said. "If she steps uneven—"

"She won't," I said. "We plowed last spring and leveled the near pasture. Besides, I'll just walk her, and I'll watch every step."

Finally he nodded, and I left the paddock. Never had I felt more pent-up energy in a horse. Melly would have loved to take off and run like her wild ancestors, free in the grass and trees. That's what I would have loved too. But that wasn't what I was getting paid for.

Melly pranced along the outside of the paddock. Her head made little turns in the direction of the starting gate, as if she knew she was bound to do battle with it, and she was scoping out the opposition.

"Don't be afraid," I told her. I urged her within a few yards of the starting gate. "Come on, Melly," I coaxed. "We're just going to walk by it, in front of it. See?"

Cautiously, Melly set one foot down, then the other, until we were just a couple of feet from the gate. Suddenly she snorted. I felt her tense and gather her neck and body as if they were elastic. With one ferocious move, she reared up and pawed at the monster.

I was too slow to react. I reached for the mane, but hers was too short. There was nothing to grab on to. I felt myself slipping down the long slide of her back, flailing through blurred air until I pounded the ground and everything went black.

9

I couldn't have blacked out for more than a few seconds, just long enough for every last ounce of wind to be knocked out of me. I forced myself to open my eyes and gasp in air. A black blur streaked in front of me, and the sound of hooves on dirt pounded in my ears. Then Orphan came into focus, rearing at Melancholy Baby, as if to ward off an attack.

"Easy, Orphan," I said, sitting up too fast. Everything spun out of control, but I could see Melly standing a few feet from me, her head lowered, her eyes sad. "She didn't mean it, Girl. Easy, Orphan."

"Scoop!" Charley knelt beside me and put his arm around me, supporting my back. "Are you all right? Should we phone for an ambulance? Don't move."

Before I could answer him, Maggie 37 was at my other side, stroking my hair. "Scoop, are you okay? Are you hurt?"

"Only my pride," I said, getting to my feet. I shook myself and made sure nothing felt broken. "It was totally my fault," I said. "I should have stayed away from the starting gate." I scratched Orphan behind her ears. "Thanks for coming to the rescue," I murmured. Reaching out with my other hand, I stroked Melly's head and scratched her withers until her eyes closed.

"Melly doesn't look dangerous now," Maggie said.

"She's not at all dangerous," I said. "Did you see the way she froze the minute I fell off? She didn't move. She didn't want to step on me."

"I'm so sorry about this," Charley said. "I'll stable her for you." He took a step toward Melly.

"No way!" I said, taking hold of Melly's reins. "Never quit on a miss." It was something my grandad used to say. When I fell off one of his horses, he didn't care how badly I was hurt. I had to get right back on so the horse wouldn't think he could throw people any time he wanted to.

"But shouldn't you go see a doctor or something, just in case?" Charley asked, his face twisted in worry.

"For that?" I said. "I promise. I've had the wind knocked out of me so many times. I know that's what happened. If I'd hit my head, or if I'd done anything but knock the wind out of me, I'd stay down until they carried me away in an ambulance. So, will you give me a boost up, please?"

"You actually want to get back on her, without a saddle?" Charley asked.

"There's no use arguing with her, Charley," said Maggie. "Not when it comes to horses."

We led Melly farther away from the starting gate. This time, as if she wanted to make up for throwing me, she stood perfectly still while I mounted her. "Okay, Melly," I said. "Let's explore a little and forget all about that iron monster."

Melly walked flat-footed for me all around the pasture, and Orphan trailed right after us. About halfway across the field, Misty darted out and joined the parade, dancing around Orphan as we circled the pasture. We rode into the paddock and circled at a walk, then a trot. I brought her into the middle of the arena and backed her. She didn't like it, and tried to catch her bit between her teeth. It took three tries to get her to take one step backward.

"You don't need to back her," Charley said. "Besides, we don't want her backing out of the gate or anything."

"I think backing up may be her control point, Charley," I explained. "I believe every horse has a favorite petting spot. I discovered Melly's while she was still in the trailer. She loves to have her withers scratched. Orphan would rather have me scratch her cheek. Moby likes being stroked high on her neck.

"I still don't get it," Charley said.

"Okay." I tried again. "I also believe each horse can have a control center, something they hate to do or give up to the rider. If I discover what that is—whether it's doing a slow walk, standing stock still, or doing pivots—I get the horse to respond and turn that power or control to me. Melly hates backing up on command. If I can get her to give in to me and back up when I ask her to, I think I have a good shot at talking her through the starting gate."

Charley raked his thick, black hair with his fingers. "Well, give it a try then."

As I worked with her, Melly responded more and more readily, finally giving in to the slightest pressure of my hand asking her to back up.

"Scoop," Maggie said, coming up to us and stroking Melly's shoulder, "I'm going to be late for play practice. Do you care if I take off?"

"Go on, Maggie," I said, swinging my leg over and jumping off Melly. "I'm done anyway. Thanks for helping."

"Do you think she'll be ready to try the starting gate tomorrow?" Maggie asked.

"We'll find out," I answered, wondering the same thing.

"I have to go too," Charley said, handing me Melly's halter and lead rope. He wrapped up the long lunge line. "I can give you a lift if you need one, Maggie. Scoop, are you sure you don't need us to help get Melly cooled?"

"Scram," I said, slipping off Melly's bridle and slipping on her halter. "Melly and I want to be alone."

I led Melly around the paddock to cool her off, although she hadn't even broken into a sweat. Charley and Maggie drove off honking and waving. On the third trip around the ring, something on the other side of the fence caught my eye. Wedged between the fence post and a rock was one of the missing brushes. It made me mad all over again. The brush was squished and dirty, making me hope I didn't find the other ones.

I played with the filly for a while, tossing her the beach ball we keep at the barn just for horseplay. When I looked at the sky, the sun was low at the horizon. Dusk swept in as a gray cloud passed over the sun, casting a long shadow over the paddock. Suddenly the day caught up with me, and a tiredness seeped into every bone. Once more around the paddock, I told myself, and I'm going home to sleep.

In front of the barn a car door slammed.

"Jen? Travis? Is that you?" I'd been half-expecting them all day, hoping nothing had gone wrong with Jen. Crossing the paddock to meet them, I called, "Hey! Jen, I thought you guys—"

"Hardly." Instantly, I recognized the voice of Stephen Dalton. He walked up to the paddock fence with Ursula and her brother Lawrence. "We were in the neighborhood, and here we are." Ursula had a dress on, long, red, silky, with a Chinese collar. Lawrence and Stephen both wore ties.

I kept walking Melly, while Misty and Orphan held their ground in the center of the paddock and kept an eye on us.

"Impressive speed, Sarah!" Stephen yelled. He's one of the only one who calls me Sarah, and he does it to drive me nuts. It works.

Ursula and Lawrence laughed as if Stephen's comment was the funniest thing they'd ever heard. "Larry," Ursula said, flipping her long, blonde hair over one shoulder, "this is Sarah Coop."

"We've already met," Lawrence said.

"Oh that's right!" Ursula exclaimed. "Thanks to me and my directions." It was obvious they'd already had a good laugh at Horse-feathers' expense.

Melly was cooled down enough and ready to go in her stall. I forced a polite tone and asked them, "Is there something I can help you with?"

"We just dropped by to check out the competition," Stephen said. "This horse doesn't look all that fast to me."

"This isn't the horse Dad was talking about," Lawrence explained. "Jacksonian's Justice is a colt, a 3-year-old. He's favored in Friday's race.

91

What's this horse's name?"

"Melancholy Baby," I said, getting more and more anxious for them to leave. I wished Maggie had still been around—or even Charley. It felt too much like three against one.

"Melancholy Baby. That's it," Lawrence said. "I think this filly is still a maiden, isn't she?"

I thought I remembered Charley saying a maiden is any horse that hasn't won yet. But I couldn't be sure, so I just shrugged. "I wouldn't be so quick to count this horse out if I were you," I said. I hated the way they looked down on Melly. I wondered if that was how Charley felt when his dad took Storm for granted.

"You know," Stephen said, pretending to talk to Ursula, but saying it loud enough for me to hear, "doesn't that lead rope look just like the ones at Dalton Stables?"

I glared at him. But I could feel my face heat up, and I hoped I wasn't blushing.

Lawrence didn't seem to hear them, although I couldn't see how he could have helped but hear them. "You may be right about that filly, Sarah," Lawrence said, eyeing Melly.

"Scoop," I corrected.

"Scoop. She's one beautiful horse," Lawrence admitted.

"Too bad it's not a beauty contest," Stephen said.

Ursula laughed so hard she had to grab

Stephen's arm to keep her balance.

"Will Fitz be entering the filly in the claims stake?" Lawrence asked above Ursula's cackle.

"I don't know what that means," I admitted.

Lawrence didn't look at me like I was stupid. Instead, he explained, "The claiming race is where owners enter horses for a specific price. People can buy the horses before the race. It's a way to help classify horses and keep the competition fairly equal. Fitz would probably enter Jacksonian Justice in the same high claiming race as we're entering Langhorne's Lucky Lady. They'd both get a good price if they sold. Melancholy Baby would probably belong in a lower claiming race because she hasn't won. Get it?"

I shrugged again. I got it, but I didn't like it. I hoped Fitz wouldn't enter Melly in any claiming race, high or low.

"Anyway, I heard that all three horses are entered in the same race Friday." Lawrence didn't sound threatening or anything. He just said it matter of factly.

Melly sneezed and shook her head, splattering Ursula with saliva.

"Hey!" Ursula screamed, stepping back and bumping into Stephen. "That horse! Look what it did!" She wiped at her red dress.

"Sorry," I said, but I was choking trying to keep from bursting out laughing.

"You did that on purpose!" Ursula wailed.

"I didn't do it at all," I said.

Stephen dabbed at Ursula's dress with a handkerchief.

"Stop it!" she shrieked. "You're making it worse! I can't go to the club looking like this!"

"We better go," Lawrence said.

"We're having dinner with the Hillsboroughs at the Kennsington Jockey Club," Stephen said. "Hillsborough is the head steward at County Downs, in case you didn't know."

I didn't know. Or care.

After they drove off, I brushed Melly and settled her in her stall. I was putting away brushes when a thud came from one end of the barn. B.C. dropped from the loft a few feet behind me.

"B.C.!" I shouted. "You scared the life out of me."

"Did not," he said, scowling.

"How long were you up there spying?"

"Was not," he said.

He was using a long stick to draw in the loose hay on the floor. The stick was as long as a horse's tail and looked like a hickory branch.

"B.C., you shouldn't jump with a stick in your hand. You'll poke your eye out."

"Will not," he said.

There was something funny about the end of the stick. "Let me see that stick, B.C.," I said, stepping toward him.

He backed up. "No! It's mine."

"I don't want to keep the stupid stick," I said, trying not to lose my temper. "I just want to see it."

"No."

I made a grab for the stick and caught the end with one hand. B.C. jerked it hard. "Stop it, B.C.!" I yelled. I looked at my palm, and it was black. Something had rubbed off on me. I lifted my hand and sniffed. It smelled like charcoal.

"What have you got, B.C.?" This time I lunged for the stick and jerked it out of his hand.

"Mine! Mine! Mine! Mine! Mine!" B.C. screamed.

Examining the end of the stick, I could see it was charred. My mind flashed back to when B.C. was in the third grade and nearly burned down his school. Somehow he'd gotten hold of a box of matches. The principal suspended him for two weeks after he set his classroom window curtain on fire.

"Benjamin Coop," I asked, forcing my voice to sound calm, "Have you been messing with matches again?"

10

"No!" B.C. yelled at me. "I didn't have matches! Give me back my stick!"

"Oh," I said, "so it is your stick?"

"Yes! Gimme it!"

"If it's your stick, and if somebody burned part of it, then who do you think did it?"

"I don't know!" B.C. screamed, leaping and grabbing for the stick I held above his reach. "I found it!"

"This isn't a game, B.C.! Do you want to burn the barn down? Because that's what's bound to happen if you start up with the matches again. I can't believe you—"

"You never believe me!" B.C. screamed. "Nobody ever believes me!" He turned and ran out of the barn.

I felt so worn out, I couldn't have run after him if I'd wanted to. Holding the stick by its unburned end, I drew back, then flung it as far away as I could.

From out front came the crunch of tires on gravel. Praying it wasn't the Dalton crew again, I walked to the front of the barn. Travis and Jen drove up in Travis's old pickup. A flock of crows in an old cottonwood tree across the lane sounded like they were fighting or having a party. I wanted to go home and fall into a deep sleep, but I wanted to see how Jen was doing.

I opened the cab door, and Jen stepped out. "Sorry we're so late," Jen said. "It's Travis's fault for letting me sleep so long. I told him to wake me up at three o'clock. I'll bet you're already done with the training."

"It's okay," I said. "You didn't miss much. I didn't even ride Melly into the gate yet." I didn't especially want to tell Travis I'd gotten dumped already. "I could really use your help tomorrow or the next day though. I have a feeling this is going to take all of us."

"Am I too late for a quick ride on Cheyenne?" Jen asked, glancing at the darkening sky.

"Never," I said. "I'll turn on the paddock light and get Cheyenne saddled."

"I can saddle my own horse, thank you very much," Jen said.

Jen went for her bridle, and I started out to get Cheyenne, but Travis put his hand on mine. I turned and looked into his deep, blue eyes, so full of concern for his sister. I knew exactly what he was asking. I put my hand on his. "It's okay, Travis."

97

He nodded, sighed, and squeezed my hand. I don't think I'd ever felt closer to Travis than right then, as we shared something deeper than words. I'd heard kids at school say that Jen Zucker had been dealt a "bad hand" in life by getting such a serious illness while she was so young. But Dotty says that God makes things work out. He balances stuff out for a person. Jen Zucker may have been given the world's worst kidneys, but she sure got the world's best big brother.

Travis carried out the saddle, and I brought Cheyenne in from the pasture. Jen tacked her up Western and mounted the Paint in the paddock.

"Shouldn't we lunge Cheyenne first?" Travis whispered, as we stood in the center of the arena and watched Jen trot around the ring. "I don't want Cheyenne throwing her."

"She'll be all right," I whispered back. "Cheyenne behaves great inside the paddock. She's been doing so well anyway that she'd probably do fine in the pasture. Still, we'll stay in here with the light to be safe."

"Watch her, will you, Scoop?" Travis looked like he was watching closely enough for both of us. "Do something if that horse looks ready to spook or anything. Jen can't fall off."

"You two aren't talking about me, are you?" Jen asked as she and Cheyenne walked by. "You know I do not like being discussed."

"Aye, aye, Captain Jen!" Travis shouted.

As if Cheyenne knew the frailty of her rider, the mare performed perfectly, obeying every command from Jen.

"Isn't Cheyenne wonderful!" I said.

"I think all our horses are wonderful," Travis said. "I want to try to get down here and ride Angel tomorrow ... unless that upsets the great race horses. I have to admit, Scoop, I still don't know why you're taking on those high-strung creatures."

"Hey, don't be too quick to judge them," I said. Travis and I exchanged grins. Those were the exact words Travis had used on me over a dozen times, only he always meant it about people: Don't be too quick to judge.

"Seriously, Travis," I said. "Just wait 'til you meet Melly. Melancholy Baby. She's a doll! She'd fit right in here at Horsefeathers. She really would."

Jen chimed in on our conversations whenever she passed. "Why don't you bring Melly out where we can see her? You could turn her loose in the pasture until I'm done riding."

"I wish!" I said. "The owners and trainers never turn these horses out. They'd kill me. They want the horses to have all that pent up energy to spend on the race. I don't get it, but I guess it's scientific or something. It must work."

Jen brought Cheyenne into the center and

pulled her up between Travis and me. "Well, whatever race horse trainers are doing, it's not so scientific and great. Did you know that in spite of all the scientific breeding and training and money, race horses are slower than they used to be?"

"How do you know that, Jen?" I asked.

"Lots of track records are half a century old. The Derby's record was set in 1926."

"No way!" Travis said. "Even at school, track records are broken every year. Runners keep getting faster and faster."

"Not race horses," Jen said.

I yawned, then tried to cover it.

"Ready to call it a night, Jen?" Travis asked. "I get the feeling Scoop could use a good night's sleep."

We took care of Cheyenne. Then Jen and Travis helped me fill the hay sacks. Our own horses chose to take to the pastures as we closed in the Thoroughbreds. "Don't you think Melly is kind of like one of ours?" I asked them, as the filly stuck her head out to be scratched.

"Careful, Scoop," Travis warned. "She's only going to be here for a couple of weeks. Don't get too attached."

"Easier said than done," I muttered.

Travis dropped me off in my driveway. I waved good-bye as he backed out and drove off. A golden glow came from our house, as if it were lit by candlelight. I knew better. It was just the yellowed window shade pulled down. Behind it, I could make out Dotty's thick shape passing through the living room.

Taking the front porch in two steps, I walked in. "Dotty! I'm home."

Dotty shuffled out of the kitchen, her feet staying flat on the floor so her open-toed slippers wouldn't come off. "Scoop, you're late. We done ate already, but I left supper on the table for you."

"Where's B.C.?"

Dotty shook her head. "He ate two bites, said two words, and closed hisself up in his bedroom. I was hoping you could tell me what went wrong on him. I seen it on his face soon as I set foot in the house."

"I didn't do anything to him, Dotty," I said. "But I did get angry at him at the barn. That's probably it." My aunt didn't need to worry any more than she already did about B.C. I didn't think he'd fool with fire again. But if I did catch him with matches, I'd have to tell Dotty soon enough.

"You reckon you could look in on him?" Dotty asked.

I nodded and headed for his room. The door was cracked open, and I stepped in. Tommy Zucker was right. B.C.'s room really was too small for more than one person. The bed against one wall took up the whole length of what used to hold a washer and dryer. Width-wise, there was barely room to turn around.

B.C. sat on the floor facing the corner, his back to me. His shoulders jerked in tiny twitches as he sniffed.

"B.C.," I said softly, "are you okay?"

His sniffs turned to sobs that shook his whole body.

"Horsefeathers, B.C.," I said, so tired I could hardly stay on my feet. "I'm sorry I yelled at you. But I couldn't have you burn down—"

B.C. wheeled around on me. "You don't believe me! You never believe anything I say!"

"That's not true, B.C.," I said. But I knew it was half true. Sometimes I believe what he says. But I didn't believe him this time. I knew he wanted me to say I believed him, but I couldn't. I didn't.

"You only believe those fancy race horse people!" B.C. yelled.

"That's ridiculous, B.C.," I said.

He looked so pitiful, pulling at his fingers as if he wanted to tear his hands right off his wrists. His face glistened with tears, and his forehead folded into tiny wrinkles and worry lines no kid his age should have.

"I wanted to ask you a favor, B.C.," I said. "I really need your help. But maybe this isn't a good time." I acted like I was leaving.

"Wait," he said, the sniffing and sobbing getting more spread out. "What? What did you want to ask me?"

"Well," I said, drawing it out so he could gather his concentration, "I'm going to need lots of help with Melly tomorrow. Don't tell Dotty because she'd just worry ..."

"What?"

"I fell off Melly today."

B.C. gasped.

"I'm okay. But that horse hates the starting gate. And I've only got a couple of days to make her like it. Think you could help me out tomorrow at Horsefeathers, B.C.?"

B.C. stared back at the corner, but the back of his head definitely nodded yes. And that was all I could get out of him for the rest of the night. Dotty and I took turns listening at the key hole or peeking in. Bottle caps clinked together all evening, but B.C. never said another word.

After making myself a tuna sandwich, I phoned Carla. She'd been staying away since Horsefeathers had gotten the race horses.

Carla's dad answered. "Hello? Buckingham residence. Edward Buckingham speaking." At least he hadn't said Edward Buckingham the Third. He'd loosened up a lot since Carla's mom had gone back to Kentucky and left ex-husband and daughter on their own. But I still had trouble getting words to come out of my mouth when I was anywhere near him.

"Um, I ... er ... is ... ?" I stammered.

"Scoop, is it?" he asked. "You would like to speak with Carla? One moment please."

While I waited, B.C.'s light went out, even though he hadn't left his room all night, not to take a bath or to brush his teeth or even to go to the bathroom. Dotty trudged by me, pantomiming that she was going to take a bath and go to bed. Her thick fingers turned an imaginary water faucet and she fake-scrubbed her arms. Then she laid her head on her folded hands and closed her eyes. I got it.

"Night, Dotty," I said.

The phone on the other end of the line clunked and crackled. Then I heard Carla's voice. "Hi, Scoop. How did it go with the race horses today?"

"Could have been better," I said.

"Huh?"

I'd forgotten how hard it was to talk to Carla on the phone when she couldn't read my lips. I raised my voice and tried to make it short. "I need you at Horsefeathers tomorrow, Carla. Can you come?"

B.C.'s door cracked open. "Shhhh!" he hissed. I glanced over just as he slammed his door shut.

"I guess I can come," Carla said.

We said goodnight, although I wasn't sure if

she'd heard mine or not. I didn't want to risk the wrath of B.C. by shouting it.

That night as I lay in bed, the moon lit my dresser in long, pale fingers of light that touched my glass jars. Each jar sparkled as if it were filled with water instead of air, air of a moment in time that I'd captured.

Collecting air was the best thing my grandfather passed along to me, and he didn't even do it until after his funeral. After Grandad died, I discovered shelves of jars we'd all believed were empty. But they weren't. Grandad had saved air in jars his whole life, labeling them so he'd remember. He had air from the day Pearl Harbor was bombed and air from the day my dad was born, air from sunsets and storms, marriages and funerals.

I'd already collected almost a dozen jars of air, carefully labeled and dated. As I drifted to sleep, I prayed to God as I did every night, imagining my room being folded in—the moonlight and the window, the A-frame roof, my horse lamp and horse posters, my dresser with the "horsefeather" Carla had given me, and jars and jars of air. Then I gave everything and everybody, every moment, back to God, with special prayers for Dotty and B.C. and Orphan— my family. Just before the Amen, I threw in Melly because in spite of Travis's warning, Melancholy Baby was feeling like family.

11

Tuesday morning I woke up as excited as if I were a jockey about to ride in my first race. With only three days left to work with Melly before her first County Downs event, I couldn't waste any more time.

I roused B.C. out of bed and knew right away he'd slipped toward the depressed end of his manic depression. He didn't say a word to me, didn't change expressions, but he did what I told him to—washed up, changed clothes, ate part of a bowl of Tastee O's cereal.

"You two be real careful today around them fancy horses," Dotty said, tugging at her nylon knee-highs and straightening her Hy-Klas employee nametag. "I won't be home 'til supper. Scoop, if you get here before me, you could make up some of that there macaroni B.C. likes so much. You'd like that, wouldn't ya, B.C.?"

B.C.'s face hovered over his cereal bowl. He didn't answer Dotty.

"And I'll get Mr. Ford to get me his best box of chocolate pudding!" Dotty's voice sounded cheery, like we'd be coming home to Christmas. "I'll betcha if I asks real nice, I could get Lou to put up some of them pistachio puddings too. You think?" She hugged B.C.'s shoulders from behind the chair. "Take care of my little man today, Jesus. Remind him how much You love him. Don't get stepped on."

B.C. and I don't have trouble sorting out Dotty's talking to God and talking to us. I was pretty sure my brother knew he was the one supposed to keep from getting stepped on and God was the One supposed to take care of B.C.

On the other hand, I wasn't sure if Dotty's words were even making it to B.C.'s brain. I wished I hadn't told him I needed him at Horsefeathers. I'd have enough on my hands there without worrying about my little brother.

After Dotty left, I turned on the TV to lure B.C. into staying home. Then I pulled on my boots, braided my hair in one long braid that hung over my left shoulder, and eased out the door. B.C. didn't say anything as I left. But when I got to the end of the driveway and looked back, my brother was following me.

Horsefeathers was already busy by the time we got there. The trainers jogged Jackson and Melly around the paddock. Charley was galloping Storm. Fitz stood in the middle of the mayhem, a king commanding his subjects. He waved for me to join him.

"Why if it isn't the horse whisperer herself! Just what we need to brighten the place and bring us luck!" Fitz hollered as I came out of the barn.

"Morning, Mr. Fitzsimmons!" I called, walking out to him, dodging between Jackson and Melly as they pranced by. I could smell their sweat and figured they'd been at it for a while.

"It's 'Fitz'!" he replied. "I'm glad to see you on this beautiful morning!"

He was right. The morning shone bright green from the grass to the trees to the stable blankets, and the temperature was so perfect I hadn't even noticed it. I wouldn't have wished for one degree colder or one degree warmer. I stood beside Fitz, trying not to notice the way his white turtleneck shirt made his stomach stick out over his belt. Maggie had called him "portly." I thought he looked a hundred times nicer than Ursula's father, even though Mr. Langhorne was as thin and fit as his son.

"And who is this young man you've brought with you?" Fitz pointed to the barn, where B.C. was leaning against the doorpost. Charley pulled Storm up to us and glanced where his father was pointing.

B.C. scowled and acted like he hadn't heard the question.

"That's my little brother, B.C.," I said, half of me wanting to rush in and make excuses for him, explain that he's manic depressive and it wasn't going to be a good day for him. But the other half of me wanted to change the subject and hope B.C. went home on his own.

"Hey there, Sport!" Fitz bellowed. "Come and tell Fitz what B.C. stands for!"

B.C. didn't budge. He dug the toe of his tennis shoe into the dirt and twisted his hands.

"It stands for Bottle Cap, doesn't it, B.C.," I said, sounding too much like Dotty when she's trying to cover B.C.'s silences. "Our dad used to bring B.C. home a pocketful of bottle caps every night after his shift at the bottle plant. My brother must have hundreds of metal bottle caps."

"Oh I see!" Fitz said, still cheerful. "And is your father still employed at the bottle plant?"

I shook my head. Out of the corner of my eye, I caught B.C. peeking over at me.

"Moved on to better things, has he?" Fitz asked.

"He's dead," I said, pretty much cutting off that conversation. "Looks like your trainer is done with Melly. I'll go see if I can help." I walked off as fast as I decently could. B.C. fell in behind me when I got to the barn.

Without speaking the same language, the trainer and I communicated pretty well. I was glad he didn't speak much English. At least he couldn't ask me questions about my parents.

Manny let me unsaddle Melly. I handed the featherweight saddle to B.C. to put away. Then I led Melly out to be cooled off. Charley was waiting for me just outside the barn.

"Scoop," Charley said, "I'm sorry. Dad's sorry. He didn't mean—"

"He didn't do anything," I said, wishing I'd never mentioned the accident to Fitz, wishing they'd drop it. "It's okay. It was nine years ago."

"I ... well ... Dad and I both think you're amazing to do all this by yourself. Did your mother remarry?" He slapped his forehead. "There I go again! I'm sorry, Scoop. It's none of my business. I was just wondering if you had any help with Horsefeathers." Charley sounded so nervous, it made me want to put him at ease, the same way I wanted Melly to take it easy.

"B.C. and I live with our aunt not far from the stable. Our mom and dad both died in a bottle plant explosion." Charley's hand covered his mouth. "Don't look so upset, Charley. It's okay. We get along fine. And I do get a lot of help at Horsefeathers. You met Jen and Maggie already."

Charley smiled, obviously grateful to have something to smile about again. "Maggie 37. How could I forget?"

"You'll probably meet Carla today. We all chip in and keep Horsefeathers going. It works out."

I cooled Melly while Storm and Jackson finished their workouts. When Charley and Julio started cooling down their mounts, I walked Melly to the front of the barn. Leading the filly past the Fitzsimmons Farms horse trailer gave me an idea. Melly hated trailers and loading for the same reason she hated the started gate—claustrophobia.

"B.C.?" I called. I looked around until I spotted him on the barn roof. I motioned him down, and in seconds he was beside me. "Put the tailgate down, B.C.," I said. "I want to load Melly."

He looked at me like I was crazy, but he jiggled and worked the latch until the tailgate ramp banged down. Melly shied to get away from it.

"Come on now, Melly," I cooed. "You trust me, don't you?" I scratched her in her favorite spot above the withers. "That's it." Step by step, I led her closer to the trailer, stopping to scratch her if I sensed her tense, then going again when she relaxed. By the time we reached the ramp, all the fight was gone out of her. She followed me right into the trailer.

Outside I heard clapping. I peered through the air cracks in the trailer and saw Fitz and Charley giving Melly and me a standing ovation. Embarrassed, I stayed where I was with Melly for a few minutes, soaking up her friendship as she nuzzled me. Then she backed down the ramp like a trouper.

Charley strolled up to us and stroked Melly's long neck. "Well, she may not get over being gate shy, but if she loads like that, you've earned every cent of the money Dad's paying you."

A horn beeped, and Fitz waved from his jeep as he drove off.

"Dad's got an appointment or something," Charley explained. "I can stay and help you with Melly if you need any help."

Something fell at our feet—bottle caps. I looked up to B.C. on the barn roof again and shook my head hard at him. I knew he wanted to be the one to help me with Melly. He was already resenting Charley.

Before I could answer Charley or yell at B.C., another horn honked. Travis and Jen Zucker drove up the lane, with Maggie 37 and Carla in the back of the truck. It looked as if I'd be getting all the help I needed.

During the rest of the day, I learned a lot more about racing and starting gates than Melancholy Baby did. Charley tacked up Melly like she'd be for the race on Friday Then I climbed into the saddle, my legs bent in two, the stirrups so short I could touch them without leaning over.

Carla hung back from the main action. She reminded me of a disapproving school teacher. "I don't know, Scoop," she called to me as I struggled to keep my shoe in the stirrup, "this is not my vision of a horse gentler. A jockey maybe, but a horse whisperer? No way." Still, Carla stuck around for an hour until Ray came by for her.

Jen had read all about starting gates, so she and Charley manned the contraption. After I'd ridden Melly in circles around the gate a dozen times, Maggie saddled up Moby, and Travis saddled Angel. Orphan hung around and watched the show.

"I think Melly's calm enough to give the gate a real try," I said, as Maggie and Travis rode out to meet us in the pasture. "B.C.!" I yelled. He'd spent the last hour watching us from an oak tree a few yards away from the starting gate. "I want you to be the leader. You can lead Orphan through the gate first. Then Travis and Maggie, you guys follow Orphan. And I'll follow you."

Orphan was so good I wanted to jump off of Melly and give my horse a big hug. She let B.C. tug and jerk on the lead rope. She followed him as calmly through the open starting gate as if she were walking through a stall on her way out to pasture.

Moby followed Orphan in a prance that made the old white mare look 4 instead of 24. Travis's Appaloosa Angel gave him a little trouble, sidestepping before he finally agreed to go into the gate. But Travis got him through.

I squeezed my knees to urge Melly toward

the gate, staying close on Angel's and Travis's heels. "Come on, Girl. It's just like the trailer, only you get to keep walking through."

Melly picked up each foot high off the ground as if the grass burned her hooves. But she followed the other horses and walked straight through the open gate.

We repeated our parade eight more times until Melly didn't change her pace, didn't tense up at all.

"I say we call it a day," Charley suggested.

No one argued with him.

"Thanks, everybody," I said. They looked as tired as I felt. But I knew it had been a great day's work. *Thanks, Lord,* I prayed, as I returned Melly to her stall. *I don't know how You feel about praying on the races. But if it's okay, I'd like to ask You to let Melly win one. She's such a good horse. And it wouldn't hurt if Horsefeathers got some of the credit. Anyway, help me do all I can do to earn a good reputation for us. Amen.*

Wednesday and Thursday flew by fast. By Wednesday afternoon Melly was standing still in the gate. Even without other horses around for her, she'd stay in her stall for as long as I asked. We practiced walking her in when the front to her gate stall was down. When we lowered her back gate, boxing her in completely, she threw a couple of fits. But once they were over, she allowed us to close her in.

Thursday morning was the first real rehearsal. Melly rode into the iron monster easily for me. Then Charley closed the gate behind us. But Melly was too smart for us. She sensed that we were up to something. I thought the filly was going to jump out of her skin.

"Easy, Melly," I murmured. I knew Julio and Fitz were watching us closely from the paddock, but I tried to block the thought of them out of my mind. I focused on Melly. I scratched her withers and talked her down until she stood, tense but still, in the tiny middle gate stall.

"Now," I whispered.

Charley banged opened the front. Melly exploded from the gate. Adrenaline rushed through my body as Melly continued in a burst of speed like I'd never felt before. I was blinded by the force of the wind as we tore away from the gate. It took me a while to bring her down to a trot and turn back to the gate.

"Uh oh," Charley said as I finally rounded back to the gate.

"What?" I asked. "Did I run her too hard?"

"No," he said slowly. "Julio didn't breeze her today in prep for tomorrow."

"Then what?" I asked.

Charley's grin spread over his whole face. "I do believe I saw the racing bug bite you."

I touched my cheek, and it felt on fire. My heart was still racing. "Maybe," I admitted.

We only tried the gate one more time because we didn't want to drain Melly's strength for the race. This time when she leaped out of the gate, I felt my soul leap with hers.

Charley was right. I had been bitten by the racing bug, something I never would have thought possible. And I could hardly wait for the real thing.

12

Although we were scheduled to leave before dawn on Friday morning, I was ready two hours early. I changed clothes twice, ending up with my best pair of jeans and a green T-shirt to match the Fitzsimmons Stable colors.

Maggie was going with us, and we'd arranged to meet at Horsefeathers and ride to the fairgrounds with Charley and Fitz. They'd agreed to let B.C. tag along with us, although I wished I hadn't promised him he could come. Dotty hadn't liked the idea of B.C. at the tracks, and I knew Fitz probably didn't either. And to tell the truth, neither did I. B.C.'s mood had stayed low the whole week. But I'd promised him, and I couldn't see any way around it.

I thought I heard B.C. stirring in his room, but I decided to let him sleep as late as possible. Dotty would have to work all day at the Hy-Klas, so I let her sleep too. After checking the kitchen clock a couple of dozen times, I wrote Dotty a note and left it on the kitchen table. Then I went to wake up B.C.

I knocked on B.C.'s door and peeked in. "B.C., it's time to get up for the horse—"

But B.C. wasn't in his bed. He was gone. I couldn't believe he'd sneaked off without me. I hurried out the door and took off for Horsefeathers, my eyes adjusting to the dark and starlight. Halfway down the drive I remembered my jar. I raced back in, took an empty pickle jar from under the sink, and stuffed it in my backpack. Then I walked in moonlight to Horsefeathers.

I should have known I couldn't beat the Fitzsimmons' crew to Horsefeathers. The horses were already blanketed. In the corner of the barn, Julio and Manny sat drinking coffee and talking fast in Spanish. I was on my way over to say hello when I heard a noise coming from the end stall, where Storm was staying.

Crossing in front of the tack box, I turned down the stallway to investigate. When I put my hand on Storm's stall door, it opened in my face. I gasped and stepped back.

It was Charley. "Are you okay?"

"I'm okay," I said, my heart beat slowing down to normal.

"I thought I heard you out here," Charley said. "I was just checking in on Storm. She probably won't race today."

~~~~~~~~~~~~~~~~~~~~~~~~~~~~~~

I felt bad for Charley. I knew how badly he

wanted to see Storm win a race. "I'm sorry," I said, not looking at him. Storm might have felt the disappointment too. In her stall, she paced and stamped. "Maybe she can race next week?"

Charley shrugged. "It's okay. Dad's bringing her along as a Lead Pony to keep Jackson steady. And she's an Eligible, so she'll be ready to race if another horse scratches."

Charley was rubbing something in his hands. When I looked closely, I could see it was a stick.

"Where did you get that?" I asked, trying to hide the fear that was creeping up inside of me. I took the stick from him, hoping I wouldn't find what I thought I'd find. But it was there—a blackened, charred tip. One end of the stick had been burned.

I touched the tip, hoping it was the same stick I'd found B.C. with earlier that week. But it wasn't the same one. The black tip on this one was still warm. "Charley," I asked again, "where did this stick come from?"

"I was going to ask you the same thing," Charley said, frowning at the burned end. "It was outside Storm's stall. I only saw it because it was still smoking a little on the end."

My chest felt tight and boxed in. B.C. was doing it all over again. I should have told Dotty when I caught him the first time.

"Are you okay?" Charley asked, bending his

head down to look at my face. "Don't worry about it. Maybe somebody was cooking marshmallows or something. I don't know."

I shook my head. If I told him, Charley might tell his dad, and they'd take their horses to somewhere kids didn't play with matches. But I didn't have a choice.

"Charley," I began, "I think it's my brother's stick. B.C. was playing with a burned stick like that on Monday. I had a talk with him. I really didn't think he'd try it again." My throat was closing in on me, so the words squeaked out thin and high. "I—I'll understand if you and your dad want to move the horses away from Horsefeathers."

"Scoop," Charley said, touching my chin, lifting it so I had to look at him. "We're not moving our horses anywhere. Don't be nuts." He carried the stick to the paddock and pitched it over the fence. When he came back, he put his arm around my shoulder. "This will be our secret, Scoop. Talk to B.C. again, and then forget it."

I could have hugged him right then and there. "Thanks, Charley. Thanks for understanding." I felt as if he'd given me another chance. "It won't happen again. Trust me!"

It took me a couple of minutes to find B.C. sitting in the hay loft. Dogless Cat was curled up next to him. The sense of relief I'd felt when

Charley threw out the stick faded like a puff of smoke the minute I saw my brother. "B.C.!" I said as loud as I dared. He didn't turn around. "B.C., I'm talking to you!"

When he still wouldn't turn to face me, I stomped across the loft so I'd be in front of him. "You almost ruined everything!" I said. "How could you do that? How could you play with matches after you promised you wouldn't?"

He frowned up at me. At least it was some kind of a response, enough to let me know he was hearing what I said.

"Why are you doing this? Don't you care about Horsefeathers? Or me? Do you want to burn the barn down?"

"I didn't do anything," he whispered.

"Don't lie to me, B.C.! I saw the stick myself! Charley found it. If he'd told his father, Horsefeathers would be out business."

"Charley," B.C. muttered, as if it were a swear word he didn't want Dotty to hear.

"Yes, Charley!" I whispered back. "You should thank him for not turning you in."

"I didn't do anything," he said, picking pieces of hay from the bale he and Dogless were sitting on.

Below came the cry, "Scoop! Dad's here! We need to get the horses ready to load!"

B.C. got up and started toward the ladder.

"Oh, no you don't, B.C.! You're not going

anywhere except home."

"You promised!" He spat the words out at me.

"And you promised not to play with matches. We're even!" I pushed past him and climbed down without looking back.

"Where's your brother?" Charley asked as he got down the lead rope for Storm.

"He's not coming," I said. "I'll get Melly."

Maggie 37 Green—in greenish-brown jodhpurs and a green, silk shirt that could have passed for jockey silks, arrived just in time to hop into the trailer with Fitz, and me. Julio, Charley, and Manny drove in a separate car.

On the drive to County Downs, my spirits gradually lifted. The farther we got from Horsefeathers and B.C., the more my excitement grew. Fitz kept Maggie and me entertained with stories of horse trading and racing.

"So the race officials began evening the playing field," Fitz was saying, "by adding weights to mounts with lighter jockeys. Nowadays they use lead weights under the saddle, but above the saddle pad. And that's where we get the expression, 'Get the lead out!'"

"I say, Fitz," Maggie said, maintaining her British accent in spite of the fact that she was laughing so hard she could barely talk. "You spin a grand yarn. I might believe you about the lead weights, but I do not believe there ever was a

'Backwards Bobby.' No jockey could stay on backwards for a mile-and-a-quarter race—and win!" She collapsed into another laughing fit.

I wondered if this was what other race people did to keep their nerves calmed. I imagined the solemn ride in Dalton's Stables trailer, or in a limo with the Langhornes. I was pretty sure they couldn't have been having as much fun as we were having.

"There it is!" shouted Maggie as the fairgrounds came into sight. "Isn't it wonderful! Glorious! Marvelous!"

I'd never been to County Downs, not the racetrack and not the fair. The first thing I noticed were yellow-and-white tents spread across an entire field. When we turned off the main road, we were greeted by white fences, a grandstand, and the racetrack itself, partially hidden behind thick, green bushes. I could make out the white fence circling the track and a big metal board in the center green island.

"I want to learn everything about racing," I vowed.

Fitz laughed. "Everything, huh? All right. Did you know that the first races were between rival desert chieftains more than 3,000 years ago in the Middle East? They kept their horses thirsty, and then let them race to the water."

"That's mean!" Maggie exclaimed.

Fitz continued. "The Greeks and Romans

were fanatics about horse racing. About 2,000 years ago, Rome had as many as a hundred races a day—complete with gambling, race fixing, bribery, horse doping, all the wonders of our modern world."

Fitz drove the trailer into a line of horse trailers waiting to get inside the grounds. After a few minutes of getting nowhere, he pulled out of line, passed half a dozen trailers, and beeped his horn at the entrance.

A man in a red velvet jacket and a tall hat walked over to us and leaned in. "Well hello, Fitz!" he said. "I heard you were coming. What do you figure your odds are against the Langhorne filly?"

"Nice to see you, Walter," Fitz said, shaking the man's hand. "I have a good feeling about the race today. Jacksonian Justice in the 3rd. But keep it under that hat, will you?"

The man waved us in, and Fitz wound past horses and jockeys, past arguing trainers, past horses in stable blankets. We were on the opposite end from the regular fair-goers, but I caught glimpses of couples holding hands, kids running, and whole families taking in the early morning exhibitions.

"This is it," Fitz said, as he stopped the trailer at what looked like a big, busy stable. We piled out. "Welcome to 'Shed Row,' Fitz said. "We can make this our home base. Our horses have stalls reserved."

Maggie squeezed my arm. "This is so exciting!" she said, losing her accent. "I can't believe Carla didn't want to come! What about Jen?"

"She said she and Travis would come next week, the next time the horses race. I think they had plans." I was pretty sure Maggie understood that when Jen said she "had plans," she usually had a doctor's appointment.

Melly unloaded easily. I led her to a large, straw-covered stall. Already the day was warming up, and the air was filled with a dozen different horse smells mingled with the scent of hay and coffee.

"What do you think?" Charley stood behind me and took in a deep breath.

I did the same. "I think," I replied slowly, my eyes closed, my face tilted up to feel the morning sunrise, "that when I hear about horse races from now on, this is what I'll smell."

We got the horses settled, groomed, and fed. Then Charley took Maggie and me on a tour of County Downs. We met horse breeders who talked faster than B.C. in manic mode, trading tips and bragging about sires and dams. Charley led us as close as we could get to the dirt track, and we watched them groom the dusty turf.

"Do those scoreboards there show the winners?" Maggie asked, pointing to the long, metal boards in the center green island.

"They're betting boards, called a 'Tote Board.'" Charley bought a racing form and showed us how each horse was favored with different odds: 3 to 1; 10 to 1.

"But the odds can change once the betting starts. Look. In the third race, Jackson is the favorite—the Chalk—at 3 to 1. Langhorne's Lucky Lady is 4 to 1, and Melancholy Baby is 7 to 1. Things will change closer to post time."

I looked behind us into the grandstand, where already spectators were sprinkled around on the bleacher seats. One man in faded gray pants and a threadbare, off-white shirt looked like he'd spent the night on the bench. He was hunched over a racing form and had newspapers spread all around him. When he looked up, I turned away.

"We better get back to the sheds," Charley said. "There's a lot to do before we can race."

I took in everything as we walked back to our horses—the nervous laughter, the thrill of anticipation, whispers over who was going to bet on what. People strolled around in dresses and suits they could have gone to the country club in. I'd never seen so many gorgeous horses in one place, each one bought as a foal for thousands and thousands of dollars. Nothing about the racing scene was seedy or ugly like I'd thought it would be. It made me proud to think that Horsefeathers was a part of it all.

13

The morning passed like a fitful dream. Everybody was either rushing to get things done, or waiting and waiting for time to pass. Maggie and I helped shovel manure. We ran errands for Fitz, running paperwork from one spot to another. We brushed horses and checked tack.

Maggie 37 had already made dozens of friends at the track. Whenever she had a question, she walked up to total strangers and asked. People loved instructing her in the fine points of racing strategy. Everywhere we walked on the ground, people called out, "Hi, Maggie!"

We hadn't seen much of Fitz since we'd hit the racetrack. He had floated in and out, spouting orders. Around noon, we met Jackson's jockey. Melly's jockey was riding in the first race, so we wouldn't have the chance to meet him until it was time to saddle up for the race.

Finally we heard the loud speakers welcoming everyone to County Downs Racetrack. Each word set off an invisible electrical current that started people buzzing with race talk throughout the fairgrounds.

Fitz ran up to Julio and motioned us over for last minute instructions. "This is it!" he said. "Let's all give it our best. We've got good jockeys and good post positions. Let's make it a great day for Fitzsimmons Farms ... " he smiled at me, " ... and Horsefeathers Stable!"

Over the loudspeaker came the announcement calling horses into the gate for the first race. After a few minutes, I heard a loud clank and recognized it as the starting gate being lifted. "And they're off!" cried the announcer. Crowd cheers swelled in an explosion of voices.

Fitz looked more serious than I'd ever seen him. "Charley," he said, "you and Storm keep Jackson calm. The odds are way down on him. He's the Chalk and may run at 2 to 3."

Charley nodded, then rode off on Storm. He skillfully kept his horse just in front and to the right side of Jackson, who was lead by Julio.

Fitz turned to me. "Scoop, once Melly's jockey is in the irons, it will be up to you. I want you to lead Melly to the starting gates."

"Me? On the race track?" Nobody had said anything about me going on the track with Melly.

"Listen, Scoop. Melly's got a good chance to win this race, or at least to beat the Langhorne filly. She's got the inside position, and she's in top form. Her odds are already up to 15 to 1. But you know and I know that Melancholy Baby is better than that. If she can break clean from the gate, she'll show them all. Will you help her?"

"Of course she'll help!" Maggie shouted. "I just wish you had Horsefeathers written on your shirt. Scoop, say something!"

Horses were stampeding in my stomach. The loud speakers blared like bombs bursting in my brain. But I managed to nod. "Let's do it."

A lot of what happened after that is foggy. On the way down to the track, I held on to Melly's reins so tightly I cut my palm. In the racing paddock, a jockey appeared, my size or a bit smaller. We shook hands when Fitz introduced us. I gave him a leg up on Melly. Horses kicked dust in my face as I waited, scratching Melly's withers to calm myself as much as to calm her.

The winners of the second race were announced, and Maggie and Fitz left to watch from his box seats.

Charley rode over on Storm, who looked beautiful, the only black in the paddock. "You'll be fine, Scoop," he said. "Just follow the Outrider, the lead official on the white horse there. The rest of us will follow you."

"Thanks, Charley," I said, feeling too numb to move, much less to lead Melly onto the track.

The bugle played, and horses were called to

the post for the third race. Melly fell in behind the lead horse, and I jogged to keep pace with her. "Easy, Girl," I murmured, wishing she didn't have her head gear on so I could see her eyes more clearly. "This is just like that gate at Horsefeathers."

As we walked toward the long, metal gate, crowd noise blanketed us in a low rumble. The real starting gate was much scarier than our practice gate at Horsefeathers, no matter what I told Melly.

"Go Scoop! Go Melly! Number One!" Somehow Maggie's shouts pierced through the crowd and reached us.

Closer and closer, we moved to the gate. I could sense Melly tense up. I reached up and scratched her withers. "If she acts up in the gate," I said, looking up at the jockey, "just do this to calm her."

He nodded, his little green and white cap bobbing.

The number two horse was on our tail. I glanced back and recognized Langhorne Stable colors and the big sorrel, Lucky Lady. But Melly kept her gaze on the starting gate. She slowed down when her nose reached the stall. Next to us, Lady slipped into her box. So did Jackson. Only a couple of horses resisted their jockeys.

"Come on, Melly," I said. I walked in front of her into the gate. "Please?"

Melly bobbed her head up and down, then followed me into the starting gate.

"Be careful down there," said the jockey. "You're dead meat if she spooks while you're still in the box."

"You won't spook, will you, Melly?" Her eyes showed white with anticipation, but not terror.

Grooms leaped out of stalls as the back door clanged down, boxing the horses into the starting gate. I slipped out just in time. A shot fired, and the announcer hollered, "And they're off!"

"Scoop! This way!" Charley motioned me to the fence, where we could watch the race. All I could make out was a cluster of horses bunched together.

The announcer called the race, and finally I picked Melly and Jackson out of the crowd. "Midnight's Mystery Man takes the lead at the gate, followed by Langhorne's Lucky Lady, Melancholy Baby, Jacksonian Justice, and Glue Gun Girl."

"They're losing, Charley! What's wrong?" I cried.

"It's okay," he said. "We don't want them in the lead yet. They'll be spent. The lead horse, Midnight, is a rabbit. He'll spend all of his energy and still have half a track to go. Don't worry. We've got good jockeys on our horses. They'll make their moves when it's time."

"Go Melly! Go Melly!" I'd never cheered or yelled like that, caught up in the frenzy of the race. Melly stayed neck and neck with Jackson, just in front of Lucky Lady, with Midnight leading the pack.

"Moving into contention are Jacksonian Justice and Melancholy Baby, both owned by Fitzsimmons Stable. On the outside it's Bet to Win, Prancing Partner, Ain't No Nag, and Jo Jo's Money! Melancholy Baby's looking for room on the inside as they head for the far turn. Langhorne's Lady won't give up that rail.

"Get out of her way!" I yelled. "Run, Melly!" The crowd roared so loud I couldn't hear myself shout.

The horses were strung out as they came around the far turn. But I could see that Midnight was fading to the back, just like Charley had predicted. Jackson had dropped to third, with Melly fighting for the lead against Lucky Lady.

"And coming into the home stretch, it's a battle, with Langhorne's Lucky Lady neck-and-neck with Melancholy Baby. Jacksonian Justice fades to the pack.

"Something's wrong with Jackson," Charley said. Jackson was running, but it looked like he was standing still as other horses flew by him. "He's never lagged like that, never just faded."

But my mind was on Melly. "Go Melly!" I

screamed, my throat aching.

As if she heard me, Melly surged one last time, stretching her neck as they thundered to the wire. Her legs looked straight, like spokes on a wheel, tearing to the finish line.

"And it's Melancholy Baby pulling past Lucky Lady as they reach the home stretch. Melancholy Baby! Melancholy Baby has it by half a length! Followed by Langhorne's Lucky Lady and Jo Jo's Money to show!"

"She won! She won!" I jumped up and hugged Charley. "Melly did it! She really did it!" I let him go, hardly realizing I'd just thrown myself into his arms.

"Did you see her?" Maggie and Fitz ran up to us. "Oh Scoop! Wasn't that amazing!" Maggie cried. We hugged each other. Then we hugged Fitz, who didn't seem very excited. Maybe people can get used to winning.

Melly hadn't stopped running at the finish line. The jockey had ridden her out and circled back. She pranced as if she knew she'd just beaten everybody and all the applause was for her.

"They'll want us in the Winner's Circle," Fitz said. "There's Melly."

I ran with Fitz onto the track. Melly was foamy and heaving hard. Saliva dribbled from her bit. I reached up and scratched her withers, which were drenched in sweat. She pranced in place.

"Excellent race," Fitz said, shaking the jockey's hand.

"We broke well," he said. "I knew we had it from the starting gate."

I felt as proud as if I'd just won the race myself. Down past the paddock I caught a glimpse of Jackson. Julio was leading him away. I felt bad for Jackson, but he'd already had his share of wins. It was Melly's turn.

I watched as the jockey rode Melly into the Winner's Circle. Fitz stood at Melly's shoulder and received a winner's plaque and a check, the winning purse. As the announcer read out the name Melancholy Baby and Fitzsimmons Stable, a woman placed a kind of wreath, but long like a scarf, over Melly's withers.

"Say a few words for us, Mr. Fitzsimmons," the announcer asked. "Isn't this Melancholy Baby's Break Maiden? Can you tell us what made the difference and gave your second horse its first win?"

Fitz took the microphone. "Scoop, will you come up here, please?"

I froze. Photographers stood ready to take Fitz's picture, but they turned now and stared at me.

"Come on!" Fitz commanded.

I felt frozen to the turf. Maggie and Charley pushed me from behind to get me going.

"We were disappointed in Jackson's performance today," Fitz said. "But I guess even the great ones are entitled to a bad day. And we couldn't be happier for our Melly."

I'd reached Fitz and now stepped behind him.

"This is Sarah Coop, known as Scoop," he said, putting his arm around my shoulder and pulling me beside him. "Scoop is as fine a horse gentler as I've ever seen. We're keeping our horses at her stable, Horsefeathers, mainly so she could get Melly over her fear of the starting gate. I think Melly's performance today says it all. Let's give this little lady a big hand."

Maggie whistled, and everybody applauded. Flashes exploded as photographers took pictures. And I felt famous.

As soon as everybody drifted away and I was alone with Maggie back at Shed Row, I ran to the trailer and pulled the glass jar from my backpack. This was one day I didn't want to forget. Twirling in a circle, my arms raised to the sky, jar in one hand and lid in the other, I captured the air of County Downs—the smell of horse sweat and hay, and the feel of victory.

Hours later we were on our way back to Horsefeathers. For the first hour of the drive, we all talked at once, going over and over the minutes and stages of the race and the final victory. Then somehow, in spite of how psyched we were, or because of it, Maggie and I fell asleep.

I didn't wake up until we bounced onto Horsefeather's Lane. The darkness surprised me. We unloaded the horses, gave them a specially prepared energy mash, and bedded them down. I took care of Melly and left Jackson and Storm to the others.

Fitz drove Maggie home, but I stayed to check on Orphan and Misty. I still had to feed the regulars, even though I was tired enough to curl up in the hay loft and sleep for a week.

Finally I checked on Melly one last time and kissed her good night on the cheek. "Thanks, Melly," I said. "I'll never forget what you did today."

On the way out I passed by Jackson's stall. Moonlight filtered through a crack in the barn and landed on his stall door. Something glistened there, like oil or grease. I ran my finger along a streak that started at the top of the stall door and oozed in a thin line to the bottom. Bringing my fingertip to my nose, I sniffed. It was a familiar smell—not oil and not grease.

I hurried to the tack box and got the flashlight. The beam made my finger shine bright red. Heart pounding I raced back to Jackson's stall and shined the light on his door. I gasped. "Jackson!" The streak dripping from his stall was blood.

14

I climbed into the stall with Jackson. His head hung low, and he didn't look up when I came in. "Jackson?" I said softly. "What's the matter, big fella?"

I examined his legs, running my hand down from his shoulder, along the cannon and pastern. Picking up each hoof, I looked for cuts or swelling. Manny had wrapped Jackson's legs in white bandages, but there was no blood on them. I checked his sides, his chest, his flanks and hind quarters. But I couldn't find anything, other than a tiny welt the size of my fingernail where the jockey had used his whip in the home-stretch.

Moving to his head, I felt under his jaw for his pulse. It was strong and normal, about 40 beats per minute. Just when I was starting to think that maybe Julio had cut his hand or something, I noticed Jackson's nose. Bright red drops of blood dripped from each nostril when he moved his head.

Tears came to my eyes, and my stomach

ached. I hugged Jackson's neck and stroked his head. Why was he bleeding? What was wrong with him? "Maybe that's why you didn't run well, Jackson," I said, stroking his long neck. "You were in pain, and we made you race."

Lord, I prayed, only then realizing I hadn't bothered to talk to God that whole day at the racetrack. *Please help Jackson. I'm sorry I wasn't listening to you or to Jackson. Show me what to do.*

Fitz! I had to get hold of Fitz. He gave me the phone number of their hotel. What did I do with it? I knew I'd written down the number at home. I had to get home and call Fitz. He'd know what to do. Then I could call Doc Vicki, unless Fitz wanted his own vet.

Hugging Jackson one more time, I ran outside and whistled for Orphan. She came trotting up, nickering and tossing her head. I swung up on her bareback. "Go!" That's all I had to say to Orphan. She read the slight pressure of my knees, read my heart, and headed home, breaking into a sure-footed canter that didn't stop until we reached Dotty's front porch. I jumped off Orphan and ran inside. "Dotty!"

Dotty sat up. She'd been lying on the couch, hair curlers sticking up like a crown, her sleeveless nightgown twisted around her knees. "Scoop? I reckon I done fell asleep waiting on you. You all right? How'd it—?"

"Dotty!" I was as out of breath as if Orphan

had ridden *me* over. "Have you seen a phone number lying around here? I need the number of some hotel Fitz and Charley are staying in. I scribbled it on a napkin, I think."

"Lord, take care of Scoop and give her peace," Dotty said. "What's wrong?"

I knocked a book off the phone table. Newspapers and candy wrappers fell to the floor. "We have to find that number, Dotty!" I cried. "It's Jackson. He didn't run well at the track. And then they left. And then I found blood. And it's coming from his nose. I have to call Fitz."

Dotty picked up couch pillows and looked under them. "You wrote it on a napkin?"

"I think so."

I caught a glimpse of B.C. peeking around his bedroom door. He looked so small and sad in his cowboy PJ's that were made for a kid half his age. I went back to searching for the number. "I can't remember the name of the motel, Dotty. I have to find the number!"

B.C.'s bare feet padded across the living room into the kitchen. When he padded back, he had a white napkin in his hand. He handed it to me without slowing down or stopping. It was the napkin with the motel's phone number. "Thanks!" I shouted.

As fast as I could, I dialed the number and asked for the Fitzsimmons room. The phone rang and rang and rang. Finally, a deep, gravelly voice said, "What? Hello?"

"Charley?" I asked.

"Yeah?"

"This is Scoop, Charley. Something's wrong with Jackson! I don't know what to do? Should I call the vet?"

A clunk sounded like he'd dropped the phone. "Hello? Scoop?" Charley sounded more awake. "What's the matter again? Did you say Jackson?" Away from the phone, he said, "It's Scoop, Dad. She says something's the matter with Jackson."

The phone clunked again. Then Fitz was on the line. "Scoop? What's going on? Where are you?"

I filled him in on how I'd seen the blood and how Jackson's nose was bleeding.

"First of all," Fitz said, "calm down. No sense getting so worked up. It's not all that unusual for a Thoroughbred racer to have a nosebleed after a hard race."

I heard Charley say something, but all I could make out was " ... never ... bleeder ... before."

"What did Charley say?" I asked. I glanced up and saw Dotty staring at me, probably praying inside. I was glad.

"Charley says Jackson doesn't have a history as a bleeder. That's a horse that bleeds during heavy exertion. But there's a first time for everything. It's probably just the small vessels or capillaries in the respiratory system. It happens."

Fitz sounded so calm. He was trying to make me feel better. "Should I call the vet? Doc Vicki Snyder would probably come right out and meet me at Horsefeathers. I could call her—"

"Nah," Fitz said. "No need. Trust me, Scoop. That horse will be right as rain tomorrow morning. Don't you worry about it. I'm sorry it spoiled your racing day. You just put it out of your mind, hear?"

I let out a deep sigh that probably traveled over the phone lines. "Are you sure, Fitz? Because I can go back down there right now to make sure he's okay. Maybe I should sleep at Horsefeathers tonight so I can keep an eye on Jackson?"

"Absolutely not!" Fitz said. "You go to bed and get a good night's sleep. We'll all sleep in tomorrow. We've earned a day off. I'll come by later and give Jackson a good lookover. Until then, you just put it out of your head."

I felt so much better. "Thanks, Fitz. I can't tell you how scared I was. I'm sorry I woke you and Charley up."

We said good night, and I hung up. The adrenaline drained out of my veins, leaving only exhaustion. Dotty walked over and hugged me. "Me and B.C. was awful worried about you."

B.C. I wondered what kind of lie he'd told

Dotty to explain why he didn't go to the races as planned. Right then, I couldn't have cared less. I was way too tired to tell Dotty about B.C. and the fire stick. I didn't even want to talk about the races. County Downs and the Winner Circle seemed a million miles away.

I sent Orphan back to Horsefeathers, then fell into bed and said a short version of my prayers. Then, as I lay there and listened to the sound of bottle caps clinking below in B.C.'s room, I tried to replay Melly's victory in my head. I tried to imagine the sound of the starting bugle, the smell of the track, but it wouldn't come. None of it seemed real anymore. I couldn't recapture the thrill of the race.

Why hadn't I paid more attention to Jackson and less attention to the fuss everybody was making over me at the Downs? Why hadn't I taken better care of the horses? Horses first—that was what Horsefeathers was really about.

I tried to sleep, but I kept seeing the blood on my finger, the blood in Jackson's nostrils. Finally I must have drifted off because I woke to a sensation of falling, as if I were falling from Melly, only she was a hundred hands high. My bed shook as I woke up.

Throwing off my sheet, I got up and dressed in the dark without any idea what time it was. I tiptoed down the stairs, not turning on a lamp until I was at the front door. I clicked on the chain that dangled from the porcelain dog's nose, Dotty's favorite lamp. With the light came a flash of B.C.'s face.

"B.C.?" I cried, my heart pounding. He was sitting cross-legged in front of the door. He was dressed in jeans and a T-shirt as if he'd been there a long time.

"I want to go to Horsefeathers," he said, with zero expression on his face.

I didn't want B.C. at Horsefeathers, but I didn't feel like being alone there either. I was afraid of what might be waiting there. What if Jackson had gotten worse during the night? "Okay," I finally said. "You can come."

Neither of us spoke as we walked in a sprinkling rain to the barn without even the moon or stars to guide us, just the smell of horses. I wanted to say something to my brother. I knew his manic depression was an illness as much as Jen's kidney disease was. Still, it was hard to know what to blame on the disease and what to blame on B.C. I couldn't let him get away with playing with matches.

I'd have to tell Dotty about the fire stick. But it wasn't going to do B.C. or me any good to talk about it now.

Orphan nickered from the pasture as we walked up to the barn. I pushed back the barn door, and B.C. went in ahead of me. He pulled on the overhead light and headed straight for

Jackson's stall. When I got there, he was staring at the black streak on the stall door.

"It's okay, B.C.," I said, wishing I hadn't let him come. "Fitz said race horses get nosebleeds after races sometimes. That's all it is. Jackson ran really hard."

But it nagged at me that the horse really hadn't run that hard, at least not as hard as usual. Otherwise, he should have won the race. I remembered Charley watching Jackson fade back into the pack and saying he'd never done that before.

I walked into the stall, afraid Jackson would be lying dead in a pile of straw. Instead, he was standing over his feed bin. Relief ran through me like warm water. "Good morning—I think, morning—Jackson," I said, stroking his neck.

B.C. slipped in beside me and pet the big bay too.

Spotting some of his grain uneaten in the trough, I said, "Come on now, Jackson. You need to eat and get your strength back after that race." I fingered the grain he'd left in the corners and pushed it to the center, where he could get it without working at it.

Something in the grain felt funny. "B.C.," I said. "Go get me the flash light." I felt through the grain again while B.C. ran out and came back with the flashlight pointed at my eyes. "Give it to me, B.C."

Shining the light into the grain, I spotted what my fingers had touched. It was a small, egg-shaped sponge, light colored, but covered with something dried and black, or red. I wheeled around to Jackson. "Hold Jackson's halter, B.C.," I commanded.

Crouching under Jackson's muzzle, I aimed the flashlight up his nostrils. One looked clear, but the other nostril was blocked. "Easy, Jackson," I muttered, sticking my index finger carefully up his nostril until I felt something spongy. I pinched it and tugged. It came out easily, bringing fresh blood with it.

The stall door banged open, and Manny stood in the doorway, his eyes huge and his hands raised. He yelled something at us in Spanish, on and on, louder and louder. B.C. covered his ears and turned away.

"Manny," I said, "stop it! What are you doing?"

But he was pointing to the bloody sponge in my hand, then pointing to Jackson's nose, dripping in blood. He grabbed my elbow and jerked me out of the stall as B.C. started his low growl that turned into a yell and rose to a scream.

Manny had me by the wrists and wouldn't let

go. He kept up a steady stream of rolling angry words as he shook me. He gave angry glances at the stall, then back to me, over and over.

In horror I realized why he was yelling at me.

"Manny!" I shouted. "No! I didn't do it!"

15

Manny glared at me, spitting out more angry words through his clenched teeth. I was afraid he was going to hurt me. He thought I'd hurt Jackson. I couldn't make him understand that I hadn't.

I tried again. "No, Manny! I didn't put those sponges in Jackson. I took them out!" I knew he didn't understand a word of it.

B.C.'s scream cut off suddenly. Then my brother came charging out of the stall to my rescue. Little B.C. jumped on Manny's back. He locked his arms around Manny's neck and wouldn't let go. B.C. screamed so loud Manny covered his ears.

Free now, I didn't know whether to run away, to pull B.C. off, or to jump on Manny's back with him.

Footsteps thundered down the stallway. Charley and Fitz ran toward us.

"What on earth is going on here?" Fitz shouted.

Manny wheeled around to face him, but

B.C. didn't let go.

"B.C.," I said softly. "You can let go now."

Charley ran up to me. "Scoop, what happened? What's going on?"

Manny was obviously giving his side of the story to Fitz in Spanish, so I gave mine to Charley as fast as I could. My shoulders shook, and it took all my willpower not to break down into tears. B.C. let go of Manny and slid to the ground like a used rag.

Charley took the sponge I held up to him. "Charley," I asked, when I'd told the whole story, "why would Jackson have sponges up his nose? I don't understand any of this. What does Manny think I did?"

Hate flared up in Charley's eyes. "That dirty, rotten—!"

He turned to his dad, who was trying to calm Manny. "Dad, did you see this?" He held up the sponge.

Manny started off in a flurry of Spanish words and finger pointing at me. I stepped behind Charley just in case.

"Sponges?" Fitz frowned at me. He looked down at B.C.

I thought Manny had convinced Fitz of whatever they thought I'd done. Their glares felt like pitchforks piercing through me, leaving me empty. "We didn't do anything!" I pleaded. "Honest!" It felt terrible just imagining that they thought I could have anything to do with causing a horse pain. Fitz would probably think of what Stephen Dalton had told him about us. He'd have to wonder if maybe we really were thieves, maybe much worse than that.

"It was the Langhornes!" Charley exclaimed. "It had to be! It would be just like them, Dad. We should have known they'd try something like this!"

"Something like what?" I asked weakly.

"Langhorne?" Manny repeated. He looked from Charley to Fitz. "Is Langhorne?" He slapped his forehead with the heel of his hand. "Ayee! Langhorne!" He gasped, then ran over and kissed my hand. "Señorita."

I looked to Charley. "I don't understand," I cried.

"Jackson was sponged, Scoop," Charley explained. "Somebody put sponges up Jackson's nostrils to hurt his respiration. When he raced, he couldn't get the air he needed. That's why he faded."

"Why would anybody do that?" I asked.

Fitz strolled over to B.C. and scruffed his hair, then joined Charley and me. "It's an old racing trick, Scoop. This is not always the nicest business, is it, Charley?"

"Langhorne couldn't stand it that we had the favorite for once," Charley said, his face tight with rage. "And we never would have known if

149

the sponges had dissolved like they were supposed to. Or been absorbed."

"But how could they do that?" I asked, amazed that anybody would be so cruel. "Isn't it dangerous?"

"Sometimes," Fitz said. "I better take that." He took the sponge out of Charley's hand and turned it in his fingers.

"What are we going to do?" I asked.

"Nothing," Fitz said.

"Dad!" Charley cried. "We have to do something! We can't just let them do this and get away with it!"

"Well, it didn't work for them, did it, Son?" Fitz said. "Melly spoiled their little plan. We came home with the victory in spite of them."

"But they hurt Jackson!" I said. "They should go to jail for that!"

"We can turn them in to the racing stewards at County Downs," Charley suggested.

"And tell them what?" Fitz asked. "That our horse was sponged? We can't prove who did it. And if the word gets out about this, it will only hurt us. You know that, Charley. By the time it circulates, our name will be gossiped around as somehow connected with dirty horse racing."

"But what if they do it again?" I said. *What if they try it with Melly?* I thought.

"Now that we're onto them, we'll be more careful," Fitz said.

I shook my head. This didn't make any sense. "Fitz," I said, "even if you can't prove who did it, shouldn't you at least make some kind of report to the stewards?"

Fitz put his hand on my shoulder. "Scoop, do you know what would happen? The track would have to conduct an investigation, and your little stable would be smack in the middle of it. Manny would have to tell them what he saw, no matter what he thinks about it now. However it came out, Horsefeathers would always be linked to race fraud. Your reputation would be ruined. No, I won't do that to you or to us."

My head was spinning. "But we didn't do anything wrong."

Charley wiped his hand down his face slowly, as if to wipe off his anger. "Dad's right," he said slowly. "We can't say anything."

"Nobody says another word about this," Fitz said. "Manny?" he called. He said something in Spanish to Manny, and Manny crossed his heart. "Scoop, do I have your word on this?"

I didn't know what to think or believe. The helpless feeling of being accused stuck to me like dust. Fitz and Charley believed me, and I thought Manny did too now. But who else would? Not the Daltons or anyone who talked to them. I had to trust that Fitz knew what he was doing. "Okay," I said at last. "I won't tell."

"Good. I'll see to Jackson." Fitz disappeared into Jackson's stall.

B.C. got off the ground and walked over to Charley and me, frowning up at us. "I didn't do anything," he said quietly. Then he turned and left the stable.

Fitz came out of the stall with a bloody handkerchief. "It looks a lot worse than it is, Scoop. Jackson will be fine. The blood vessels will heal. We'll have to scratch him from the next race though."

Charley came to life. "Does that mean you'll run Storm?"

"I suppose," Fitz answered.

"Yes!" Charley didn't try to hide his feelings. "You won't be sorry, Dad! Storm's going to surprise you just like Melly did!" He ran down to Storm's stall to tell her the good news.

"What about Melly?" I asked Fitz.

"We'll keep a close eye on her. Jackson's sponges couldn't have been in there very long. They must have been put in while he was in Shed Ally at the Downs. We'll watch Melly so close next time that nobody will get a chance to mess with her. Okay?"

I nodded. But the uneasiness didn't go away. I didn't want Melly to race again. I didn't care if she won or lost. I just wanted her safe.

"Don't look that way, Scoop," Fitz said. "We'll all come out of this on top. You'll see. Just don't talk about this to anyone. No one needs to know—that includes friends, okay? You'd be amazed how fast word spreads through the racing world. Remember, our reputations are at stake."

Later, Carla and Ray stopped by Horsefeathers and took over chores so I could go home and get some sleep. I left as soon as they got there. It was hard to talk to them about how exciting the race had been when I couldn't talk about what the Langhornes did to Jackson. I just hoped I wouldn't run into Lawrence and Ursula, or even Stephen Dalton. I didn't know if I'd be able to hold my tongue.

As I walked into the house, the phone was ringing. I grabbed it. "Hello?" I said, not wanting to talk to anybody.

"So how's the Princess of the Racing Set?" Travis asked. His voice doesn't sound like anybody else's. I think if I'd never met Travis or heard him speak, I still would have been able to match his face with his voice.

"I'm okay, Travis," I said. Just tired."

"You sound beat. Was the race as good as you thought? Maggie already called and gave Jen a play-by-play. You must have gone crazy when Melly won. Jen said you got to stand in the Winner's Circle like the owners?"

"Yeah," I said, wishing I could tell Travis about Jackson and the sponges.

"Scoop, are you sure you're okay? I thought you'd be bubbling over like Maggie, high on the races."

"It's just—" What would it hurt to tell Travis? Why did I tell Fitz I'd keep my mouth shut? I sighed. "I need to sleep, Travis," I said at last.

We made plans for the next race, on Friday, when Jen and Travis would go with me. Maggie had a role in a community production and couldn't come. Then we hung up.

I didn't think I could fall asleep, but I did—right on the couch and dead to the world until Dotty walked in for her lunch break.

"Everything come out all right with that there race horse with the bloody nose?" Dotty asked.

I'd forgotten that she knew about Jackson's nosebleed. I wanted to tell her the rest, but Fitz's warning still rang in my ear. "I guess," I said. I didn't like keeping secrets from Dotty, but it really wasn't my secret to tell.

Remembering the secret I'd kept about B.C., I decided to take care of what I could. "Dotty, there's something I didn't tell you last week that I probably should have." I followed her into the kitchen, where she made herself two sandwiches with baloney she had to cut the mold off of. Then I told her about finding B.C.'s fire stick twice. "I'm sorry I didn't tell you before,"

I said, when I'd finished giving her the details.

Dotty chewed and swallowed as she sat at the kitchen table. "That's all right. B.C. already done told me."

I was stunned. "He told you? All of it? When?"

She nodded, her mouth full of baloney sandwich and mayonnaise that oozed at the corners of her lips.

"Why didn't you ground him then?" I was amazed. Dotty is as nice as they come, but she's not short on discipline, even when it comes to B.C.

She gulped a bite down and dabbed her lips with a napkin. "Ain't no need. B.C. didn't do it."

16

"B.C. didn't do it?" I repeated Dotty's words to make sure I'd heard her right.

"No," she said. "B.C. done told me he ain't played with matches in over a year. He ain't never played with them in the barn."

"And you believe him?" Dotty believes in both B.C. and me. But she wasn't usually so easy to fool.

B.C. came out of hiding, walked downstairs, and came into the kitchen. He took his stand behind the gullible Dotty and gave me a scrunched up look that said, "Ha! See! Dotty believes me."

"Okay," I said. "Did he tell you I saw him with a burned stick? Did he tell you that?"

Dotty nodded. "He found it the first time. The second time, I guess he didn't find it. He seen it though."

"Horsefeathers, Dotty! If B.C. didn't burn that stick, who did? Because somebody did. The second stick was still warm. So don't try to tell me it was just lying around the paddock! Who

156

else could have done it?"

"B.C., he's working on that. Ain't you, B.C.?" Dotty finished her sandwich and reached back to give B.C. a squeeze. "B.C. here is like one of them private eyes on TV, Sherlock Holmes hisself."

"Well, Sherlock," I said, mocking him, "who did it? Huh? If you didn't burn the stick playing with matches, who did?"

He stared down at Dotty's empty plate and muttered, "I know, but I'm not telling."

Exasperated, I looked to the ceiling. "Right! You know, but you're not telling," I said.

"You wouldn't believe me anyway," he said, still not looking at me.

"Well you got that much right, Sherlock!"

"You'll see," B.C. said. "I'm going to get proof."

"Proof? Good," I said sarcastically. "Won't that be great." I took two steps to leave, then turned back. "In the meantime, don't you dare let me catch you playing with matches again, you hear? Especially in my stable!"

The rest of the week I didn't hang out much at my stable. If B.C. had played with matches at Horsefeathers, I probably wouldn't have known about it. I'd never spent less time there. After morning chores, I left quickly so I wouldn't have to watch workouts. I didn't go back again until the evenings, when I was sure they'd all be gone.

When Friday came around, I met Fitz and Charley at Horsefeathers to load Melly and Storm. "Are you sure you don't mind if Manny and Charley ride with Julio and me?" Fitz asked as Travis's white pickup drove up Horsefeathers Lane.

"No," I said. "It makes more sense this way. Travis and Jen and I will follow you there." I'd been relieved at the change in plans, although I wasn't sure why. Neither Fitz nor Charley had brought up the subject of sponges since Fitz made me promise not to talk about it. But I couldn't think of much else when I was around them, so it made me uneasy.

"Wish Storm luck!" Charley shouted as he climbed into the cab of the truck. "See you there!"

As I watched them circle the trailer, I prayed. *God, give me a clear vision today. Things are so confused. I don't know what to believe. And take care of Melly and Storm.*

Travis got out of the truck and walked me to the passenger's side. "There's been a tiny change of plans," he said, opening the door for me.

I stepped in and started to sit next to Jen when I saw B.C. in the space behind the seat, where Travis stores junk. "B.C.! What are you doing here?"

He grinned sheepishly.

"Sit down, Scoop," Jen commanded.

"Dotty called this morning and asked if we'd take him along." Jen laughed. "She said something about our need for a good 'track detective.'"

"Dotty didn't say a word about this to me," I muttered.

Travis got in and started the engine ... on the third try. "You don't suppose Dotty didn't say anything because she knew you'd object, do you?"

I slumped down in the seat and let Jen buckle the seat belt. Actually, B.C. had been good all week. He'd disappeared for hours at a time and kept out of my hair. "It's too late to do anything about it now. But a certain little track detective better make sure he doesn't cause any trouble."

This time our ride to the track was filled with a different kind of racing story. Jen, the walking encyclopedia, had an unending supply of knowledge. "The whole set up of racing horses goes completely against the equine nature," she informed us. "Fleeing, like from a lion say, is natural for a horse. But that's for a short distance. Horses are not made to run all out for long distances like this.

"Plus, the natural place for a horse to seek safety is in the middle of the pack. The front would be as dangerous as in back with the stragglers. But if these race horses try to stay in the middle during a race, a jockey brings out his whip. The poor horse will surge forward, convinced a wild animal has clawed its rear end."

"How hard can it be on them, Jen?" Travis asked. "Racing's been going on for a long time."

"Oh, it's hard on them all right. During a race, the horse's heart beat increases tenfold! Race horses get enlarged hearts and run the risk of internal injuries."

I wanted Jen to stop talking. All I could think of was Melly and what she'd be going through again. I didn't want to know how hard it would be on her. "There's the turn!" I said, catching sight of the familiar white fences. Some of the excitement started to come back to me. "This is County Downs. We better follow Fitz in."

I rolled down the window all the way. What I'd thought was just a morning mist had turned into a drizzle.

Walter, the race steward, greeted me as we drove in. "Horsefeathers!" he declared. "Why, if it isn't the famous horse gentler. I had three owners and two trainers ask about you. You're getting quite a reputation at the track."

Not half the reputation I'd get if they found out what really happened to Jackson while he was under my care.

At Shed Row Manny and Julio acted like prison guards, not allowing anyone near the stalls except Fitz and Charley. Fitz opened his huge umbrella, and we all gathered in as close as we could. "Well, we're in for a sloppy track," he said. "That's a given. Neither horse is a mudder, but they don't mind a bit of slop."

Charley leaned in and said, "Mudders are horses that prefer muddy or sloppy tracks. Storm and Melly will be fine though."

"Storm races in the first," Fitz explained, "and Melly has the third. Both drew near the center positions. We'll just do what we can and call it a day, right? Scoop, meet us on the track. You can lead Melly into the gate again."

Travis took charge of B.C., and Jen and I headed for the clubhouse so she could get dry. I knew Travis was worried about Jen catching a cold. Some of the medicines she was taking kept antibiotics from working, so she had to be careful. We got hot chocolate and drank it where we could see the track.

"Everything looks so different this trip, Jen," I said. Straight below us in the grandstand a dozen, mostly old, men were scattered, each holding a newspaper over his head. "Look at those men. I'll bet they just keep losing money at the track, waiting to make a million dollars. And look at the horses, Jen. They're so tense. I think they're terrified."

"Scoop," Jen said, "I thought you were really into this racing thing. Maybe it's the change of weather."

"Maybe. But I don't think so. It's like I'm seeing it through different glasses." I remembered what I'd prayed on my way to Horsefeathers that morning, that God would give me clear vision. *Thanks, Father,* I prayed. It was pretty cool that God would even come to the race track and answer prayers.

We didn't go down to the track until the rain had let up and the horses for the first race were called to the track. "Charley must be a wreck," Jen said. "He really wants his horse to win."

"I should have found him and wished him luck, I guess," I said as we made our way through the crowds and mud to the side of the track where Charley and I had watched Melly's race. "I think it means a lot to him to show his father he and Storm can be winners too. Look! There's Storm in lane four!"

"Everybody okay?" Travis had sneaked up behind us. He held up a giant umbrella he must have bought at the track. I gave him a look that let him know Jen was fine. "Where's my little brother?"

"He's playing detective," Travis said, positioning his umbrella directly above his sister. "B.C. wants to watch the race from the other side. I said he could if he met us here afterwards. I have to admit, Scoop. This is pretty awesome stuff—the crowds, the competition."

The bugle sounded. The gate clanged open, and the announcer yelled, "And they're off!"

Storm broke fairly clean, but got trapped in the pack. The announcer's words blurred together with the crowd noise. Travis and Jen and I shouted for Storm, who ran a steady fifth as they rounded the far turn. As they came to the home stretch, it didn't look like there was any way she was going to "finish in the money," as Fitz called it, taking first, second, or third.

But suddenly Storm burst out of the pack. She passed the horse beside her, the horse running fourth, and moved into third place as if she'd flown over them.

The jockey went to his whip, and I thought about what Jen had said. Did Storm feel the claw of an attacker on her rump? She closed the gap on horse number three and pulled even with him.

"She's got third place!" I screamed. "Go Storm! Hold on!"

They were racing to the wire. The leader was ahead by half a length, but Storm pulled neck-and-neck with the horse in second. And just as they ran past the wire, Storm surged ahead of it.

"Storm won second place!" I shouted, hugging Jen and Travis, who were cheering too. "We have to find Charley and congratulate him!" I started to run down on the track, but Travis put out his arm to stop me.

"Scoop," he said, "I think you better give Charley a minute."

I looked where Travis and Jen were staring. Charley was on the track, kicking the side marker, screaming at the jockey. He ran at Storm in a rage. I thought he was going to beat his horse, but Fitz headed him off and wrapped his arms around his son. Charley shook him off, but seemed to gather control. He kicked up mud again, but we could see him soften.

"There's B.C.," Jen whispered. He was standing behind a bush along the homestretch, several feet up from Charley and Fitz.

The second race went by in a blur. "Shouldn't you go find Melly?" Jen said. "They'll be starting your race any minute."

I spotted Melly and the same jockey who had ridden her the week before. Travis and Jen wished me luck, and I went down on the track and straight to Melly. She nickered when I walked up, and I felt guilty for not spending more time with her during the week.

"Hey, Melly," I said, after greeting the jockey. I scratched her withers and rubbed her cheek. She smelled like sweat and fear, mixed with something I couldn't place. "You be careful out there, Girl," I murmured. "When it's all over, I'll get you nice and comfy at Horsefeathers. And I just might sneak you out for a little romp with Orphan later. You'd like that, wouldn't you?"

Charley came up to us. "You better start for the gate," he said.

"I thought Storm was wonderful, Charley," I said. "She raced her heart out to get you that second."

"I know," he said. "I shouldn't have gotten so angry. It's just that I wanted—" He stopped and reached over to stroke Melly's neck. "Anyway, Dad said he'd enter Storm in Tuesday's race before we leave. It's not much rest, but I think she can win next time."

Melly and I followed the number four horse into the starting gate. Melancholy Baby was terrific. She did everything I asked her to, but her eyes were too wide, the pupils too tiny. I knew she was frightened. And I knew that she would be 10 times this terrified when the gate opened and the race started.

I slipped out just before the back of the gate clanged down. I made it back to watch with Charley just as the announcer yelled, "And they're off!"

Melly broke clean from the gate, taking the lead. She streaked down the track half a length in front of the pack.

"Go Melly!" I screamed.

Then suddenly, as if she were racing in a movie and someone switched to slow motion, her movements turned sluggish. Horses breezed past her. Her legs froze. She stumbled. I watched in mute horror as Melly staggered and fell onto her side in the mud.

M elly!" I heard my wail as if it were coming from someone else, someone dying. I was running past stewards who tried to stop me, past a uniformed policeman, through the mud, slipping and sliding to Melly. She still hadn't moved from her side when I reached her. I threw myself to the ground and lifted her head. Nothing moved. Not her chest. Not her eyes.

I felt frantically under her jaw, trying to find her pulse. But I couldn't find it.

"Miss, you'll have to move away," someone said. I felt his hand on my shoulder, but I wouldn't let go of Melly. Beautiful, sweet Melly. I remembered how she'd unloaded for me the first day I met her in the Fitzsimmons' trailer. I could see her walking around the pasture with me. I felt her grace as she let me ride her through the practice gate.

"I'm a vet." A white-haired man gently removed my arms from Melly's neck. He put his stethoscope under her jaw. He moved to her chest and listened.

I looked up and saw Fitz and Charley standing on the other side of Melly. I couldn't hear what the announcer was saying. Someone had won. Someone had lost. And Melancholy Baby was down.

The vet shook his head. "I'm sorry. She's dead."

"No!" I cried. I buried my head in her neck. It was still warm. She couldn't be dead. Not Melly.

I was still crying when Travis lifted me out of the mud and carried me off the track. He carried me all the way to the truck, where B.C. was huddled in back. It wasn't cold, but I couldn't stop shivering as we drove away. Jen put her arm around me, and I lay my head on her shoulder.

Melly was dead. How could she be dead?

I shut my eyes and pretended to go to sleep. Pretty soon the murmur of whispered voices floated around me.

"Travis, I don't know if Scoop can handle this," Jen whispered. "She loved Melly. Next to Orphan, I've never seen her get so close to a horse."

"I still can't believe a Thoroughbred would just fall over dead, Jen. It doesn't make sense." Travis was whispering too. "That race steward said there'd be an investigation."

They were silent for a long time as Travis turned on the windshield wipers. The thumping of rain grew louder on the roof.

"He has a whistle," B.C. said out of the blue behind us.

"A whistle?" Travis repeated. "Who? Who has a whistle, B.C.?"

"Charley. And I saw him blow it when Storm was running."

I felt Jen turn around. "You're a good spy, aren't you, B.C.?" Jen said gently.

I stayed in bed all day Saturday. Every time I thought I was all cried out with no tears left anywhere inside me, some would creep up and leak out of my red and raw eyes. Twice Charley called, but I told Dotty I didn't want to talk to anybody.

In my mind I'd replayed everything a thousand times. I'd imagined every possibility from natural causes, Melly's heart failing her, to an evil plot by the Langhornes.

Dotty made me go to church on Sunday. It wasn't as bad as I thought. Travis and Jen met me on the steps outside and gave me hugs that made me cry again. But the tears made me feel better this time.

Stephen Dalton sat behind us during the service, with Ursula next to him. As soon as church was over, Stephen leaned up and said, "That was awful at the track. You must feel terrible."

I turned around. Stephen looked like he actually meant what he said. "Thanks," I muttered. I didn't really believe that the Daltons or the Langhornes would go so far as to kill Fitz's horse. Their horse wasn't even running in the same race as Melly's.

Ursula took Stephen's arm. "I'd be so scared if they were going to investigate me. Good luck with that."

Investigate?

Stephen and Ursula strolled off, and Travis came up behind me. "Sorry, Scoop. Jen and I were going to tell you."

"Tell me what?" I asked, feeling like I might vomit.

Jen joined us. "When Charley couldn't get hold of you, he called Maggie and told her. County Downs is conducting an investigation into ... into what happened there."

"Did they find out what went wrong?" I asked, looking from one to the other of them, trying to read their faces.

"I'm not sure," said Travis. "They want to see Horsefeathers, Scoop."

"They're coming tomorrow," Jen added. "They want you to be there."

"Why me? I can't believe this is happening! What do they think they'll find at Horsefeathers?"

"Calm down, Scoop," Travis said. "Maggie already told Charley she'd be there to answer their questions. It's not like the police or anything. You don't have to be there."

I left church, went home to change clothes, and walked straight to Horsefeathers. I needed to be with Orphan, to let her do for me what nobody else could. We rode through the pastures and into the woods. We walked the stream and then made our way down dirt roads and across fields all afternoon and well into the evening.

Monday morning I put off going to Horsefeathers as long as I could. When I got to the barn, two fancy cars were already parked next to Travis's pickup. Inside were Maggie and Travis, Charley and Fitz, and three men in dress pants and short-sleeved, knit shirts.

A man with a clipboard looked up when I walked in. "Is this Sarah Coop now?" he asked.

I stood between Maggie and Travis. "What's going on?" I asked.

Travis introduced me to the men, but none of their names stuck. One of them was from an insurance company. "Scoop," Travis said gently. "They found something in Melly's bloodstream, something they can't explain. They've been asking us what you use to clean the stalls."

"What I use to—?"

"They want to know if you leave ammonia lying around for the horses to drink," Maggie said, sounding like she was ready to explode.

"I would never have ammonia around the horses!" I said.

171

"Told you!" Maggie chimed in. "Scoop took better care of those race horses than anybody ever had!"

Fitz spoke up for the first time since I'd arrived. "The gentlemen aren't here to accuse anybody."

"That's right," said the shortest of the men. "We're just trying to complete our investigation. We're almost through if you'll just bear with us."

I wondered what they'd already done, where they'd looked, where they'd been. "I want to help," I said. "I want to know what happened to Melly."

"Fine," said the one with the clip board who seemed to be the leader of the pack. "If we can see your grain room, where you keep the feed, I think we'll have all the information we need here."

"Sure," I said, leading the way to the small closet where we keep our bags of oats and feed. It isn't much of a grain room, but it serves the purpose. As soon as we open a bag of feed, we pour it into big garbage cans with tight-fitting lids. The closet holds a dozen cans easily and has a wooden box to store unopened feed.

The latch was already open. I don't keep it locked, but I always latch the door. I pulled back the door and felt my head go dizzy. Every lid to every garbage can had been left off. The whole room was a mess.

"Well, there's your problem," someone said behind me. "Careless storage. Those grains, especially high corn content, could be exposed to oxidation. Anything could come out of that."

I heard Maggie 37 behind me. "That's not our feed room! I mean, it is our room, but it never looks like that. Somebody's left the lids off. Scoop would never, ever do that!"

"What about the boy?" Fitz asked. He stood in the back, and we all turned to face him.

Charley spoke up. "Sure. B.C. I'll bet he just forgot to put the lids on or something. He's ... well, he's not quite right, you know?"

A bin of oats thudded to the ground, spilling oats over the floor. B.C. poked out from where he'd been hiding behind the bin. "I didn't do it! I didn't do it! I didn't do it!" he screamed. Then he ran out, past me, through the others, pushing them out of the way and screaming at the top of his lungs.

For a minute nobody said anything. Then Travis said, "Gentlemen, I think it's time for you to leave now."

"That's a good idea," Fitz agreed. "Let's be very careful from here on out. I've suffered a great loss. That horse may have been our top filly. But from what I'm hearing, we don't have enough to go on. We can't prove anything one way or the other. Until we have more evidence, just remember—a lot of reputations are at stake.

"We have a horse, my son's horse Storm, racing at the Downs tomorrow. I don't want a cloud of suspicion hanging over us. I'd go on home right now, but Charley has his heart set on trying his horse in the last race. After that, we're heading home and cutting our losses."

~~~~~~~~~~~~~~~~~~~~~~~~~~~~~~

After everybody left, Travis and Maggie helped me clean and straighten the food bins. They wanted to drive me home, but I insisted on walking. I needed to sort things out. On the one hand, Fitz and Charley and three important race stewards were sure B.C. was to blame. We'd even caught him in the grain room. B.C. claimed he hadn't done it, but how good was his word?

Lord, I prayed as I walked up the driveway and saw B.C. on the roof, *I need good vision again. Help me see things the way You do.*

I walked around the house and climbed the willow to the roof. As I sat next to B.C., I still hadn't had a revelation. I didn't know what had happened to Melly or to the grain bins. But as I looked at B.C.'s hunched shoulders and saw past the inside-out sweatshirt, the jeans with knees sticking through the holes, I knew my brother.

"I didn't do it," B.C. said softly, not looking up at me.

I swallowed hard and put my arm over his shoulder. "I know, B.C.," I said. "I know."

18

That night after Dotty got home, the three of us sat at the kitchen table while B.C. gave us his detective report. "I still don't know what everything means," he admitted, "but I know some stuff."

Some of B.C.'s notes didn't make much sense—like Fitz wearing one brown sock and one black, or Manny and Julio having the same kind of boots, or Charley having a whistle, or Lawrence Langhorne saying the words "after" and "laughter" weird.

But other pieces of information—clues, B.C. called them—were pretty interesting. He had racing tickets and stubs he said he found in the Fitzsimmons' trailer. Dotty and I didn't ask how or when he found them. But one torn ticket showed that somebody had bet on Langhorne's Lucky Lady to win in that first race. Someone in the Fitzsimmons' camp had bet against his own horses, even though Jackson had been the favorite.

"And I saw Mr. Fitz get money at a window

right after Melly died—like he won because she was dead."

"I don't understand," I said, trying to put the pieces together. "Fitz wouldn't get money for Melly dying ... unless he collected from an insurance company. And anyway, those windows are for betting. Why would he bet against his own horse?"

"You're asking the wrong woman," Dotty said. "I can't hardly tell you why nobody would bet nothing."

B.C. leaned back in his chair. He looked older and smarter than I'd ever seen him. I wondered if I was starting to see him as God saw him. "I'm sorry I went so long not believing you, B.C.," I said. "I guess I was too caught up in all the racing stuff. Forgive me?"

His face turned red. "That's okay. I do lie sometimes." He glanced at Dotty. "But Jesus forgives me too. And I'm trying not to do it."

"What should we do now?" Dotty said. I wasn't sure if she was asking us or God.

B.C. stood up. "There's one more clue, but you have to see it for yourself, Scoop."

"Okay," I said slowly.

B.C. grinned mysteriously. "Tonight."

B.C. wouldn't even give Dotty and me a hint about his mysterious clue until evening arrived. "We'll be investigating at Horsefeathers," he announced. "Now."

Halfway to Horsefeathers I asked, "Um, B.C., when are you going to tell me what exactly we're going to do at Horsefeathers?"

"You'll see for yourself," he answered. "But you have to do what I do and be totally quiet."

I did everything B.C. told me to do and ended up belly-down in the Horsefeather's hay loft. We snake-crawled to the edge so we could peek down and have a good view of the horses in their stalls. Only Carla's horse Ham and Jackson and Storm were spending the night inside their stalls.

It hurt to even look at Melly's empty stall. She still had hay in her hay sack. I could almost see her there, her lean neck arched as she turned to greet me. Next to Melly's old stall, Storm paced, pausing long enough to grab a mouthful of hay.

"How long do we have to stay like this?" I asked.

"Shhh!" B.C. sneezed. Then he answered me in a whisper that sounded louder than my regular voice. "It may be a long time. Sometimes it is."

I wondered how many nights he'd sneaked up here and spied. Were we waiting for Melly's murderer? Is that what he thought? For a second I was tempted to get up and leave. After all, this was only B.C., the same kid who used to accuse aliens from outer space every time he lost a bottle cap. I studied him, his eyes narrowed and unblinking as he stared directly below us and into Storm's stall.

Without moving his head or lifting his stare, B.C. whispered, "I'm glad you believe me."

"Me too," I said. Although I really did believe him about the grain room, I hadn't thought back to the burning stick. I wanted to believe him about that too.

"When I was feeling awful because everybody was blaming me for stuff I didn't do, Dotty told me the same thing happened to Jesus. Did you know they blamed Him for stuff He didn't even do and they gave Him a bad reputation and killed him in between two real robbers?" He risked a quick glance at me, and I nodded. Then he went back to his spying. "And Jesus didn't even get mad. Instead He told all those bad guys that He forgave them."

"I don't think I could ever forgive the person who killed Melly," I whispered. Dogless Cat tiptoed up to B.C. and curled up beside me.

B.C. took his gaze off of Storm and squinted over at me. "Dotty says you have to because Jesus died for everybody's sins, even theirs."

This was my little brother, the real B.C., the one people missed when they didn't look deep enough. I prayed I'd remember to look deeper too.

"What's that?" I said. I heard a car drive up

and stop. A door slammed, and in seconds we heard footsteps. My heart pounded in my ears as I waited to see who it was.

A tall figure appeared below us in the stallway outside Storm's stall. I wished I'd turned the barn light on. He opened the stall door. I scooted closer to the edge of the loft, trying to get a better look.

My elbow bumped against something, probably a clump of hay or a wad of twine. I grabbed for it and missed. Stunned, I watched helplessly as it fell to the ground inches from the figure.

"Hey! Who's there? Is somebody up there?"

I recognized the voice of Charley Fitzsimmons and started to answer him.

B.C. elbowed me, his finger to his lips. He shook his head no.

"I know someone's up there," Charley said, backing out of the stall and heading toward us. "Answer me!" He put one foot on the bottom rung of the loft ladder.

It was no use hiding. In another second he'd see us. "Charley?" I called out. "Is that you? B.C. and I are up here."

B.C. let out a groan and rolled over onto his back. Charley climbed to the loft and sat beside me, with B.C. on my other side.

"What are you doing up here in the dark?" Charley asked. His gaze darted around the loft, as if he thought we were up to some awful crime.

"We ... we weren't doing anything," I stammered. "We were ... just ... ."

"We're standing guard over Storm and Jackson," B.C. said, sitting up straight.

Charley seemed to relax. "Oh, I get it. Do you think the Langhornes would try something?" He laughed lightly. "Well then, B.C.," he said, talking to B.C. like he was 3 years old, "do you mind if I join you? This looks like a lot of fun."

B.C. didn't answer him. "Ask him about his whistle," he whispered to me.

"B.C., that isn't—" Then I changed my mind and looked at Charley. B.C. was right. Charley did have a whistle around his neck. It was small and gray, and it dangled on a string around his neck. When he caught me looking at it, Charley stuck the whistle under his shirt.

"Could I see your whistle, Charley?" I asked.

Charley laughed. "This? It's silly. The thing doesn't even work. It's my good luck charm."

"Could I see it?" I asked again.

Charley shrugged. Then he took it from around his neck and tossed it to me. I missed, and the whistle fell in the hay on the other side of B.C.

"Shhhh!" B.C. held up his hand to stop us. "Somebody's coming."

Charley and I got down on our stomachs and edged up to see better. This time I was careful not to knock anything down. The barn was even darker than when Charley had come in, but whoever was down there didn't turn on the light. A thin streak of moonlight pierced through Storm's stall, providing us with the only light.

"Look!" Charley whispered, as a figure came into view and stopped outside Storm's stall. It was hard to make out, but the black outline of whoever was down there looked bigger than Charley's shadow had.

We watched in silence as the dark shadow seemed to envelop Storm's stall, opening the door and slipping in. Once inside, he turned and lifted his hand to shut the door. The moonlight sliced across his shadow and reflected off something in his hand.

Charley gasped. In a hoarse whisper he said, "It's a syringe!"

Before I knew what was happening, Charley was on his feet and halfway down the ladder. I sprang up as he jumped the rest of the way down, landing only a foot from the attacker. "Stop!" Charley screamed. "Get away from my horse!"

"Stay here, B.C.!" I ordered. "I mean it. If anything goes wrong, you run for help!"

I tore down the stairs and raced to Storm's stall. I was almost there when I heard a cry that sounded like Charley had been hurt, worse than hurt, pierced through the heart, a cry mixed with moaning.

"Charley!" I shouted, flinging back the door to Storm's stall. Charley was standing still. He wasn't hurt. His gaze was fixed on the attacker.

I turned to face the attacker, somehow knowing what I'd see.

"How could you?" Charley wailed. "Oh, Dad, how could you?"

19

"Fitz?" I said, shocked by the vision before me. Frederick Fitzsimmons stood next to Storm. In his hand was a loaded syringe with a long silver needle.

"Charley! I wondered where you were. Listen to me," Fitz said, ignoring me. "Let me explain. What I'm doing is for the both of us. You have to understand, Son. I've made some bad bets. I owe people."

"It was you," Charley said, his face contorting as if he couldn't stand the sight of his own father. "You did it all."

"I only meant to slow down Jackson. That's all. His odds were so good to win that I had to bet on another horse with longer odds. Don't you see? I bet all I had on the Langhorne's horse. I was sure it would win. If Melly hadn't spoiled everything by crossing the finish line first, that would have taken care of everything I owed."

"Melly." Charley wasn't looking at his father. He said the word as if he were in a state of shock.

Fitz kicked the straw, and Storm jerked back. "I had to, Charley. I bet what I had against Melly, but I knew it wouldn't be enough. I needed the insurance money. After Melly's win, I increased her policy. Don't look like that, Son. That horse never felt a thing. I injected her with a small amount of ammonia before the race. She never knew what hit her."

Charley finally turned and looked directly at his father. It was as if I weren't even there. "And you were going to do the same thing to my horse?"

"They'll think it was something Storm caught here at Horsefeathers," Fitz said.

"You're the one who left the grain bins open!" I said, suddenly seeing things clearly.

"I'm sorry about that, Scoop," Fitz said. "Nothing personal. I just needed somewhere like this to create reasonable doubt."

Somewhere like this. How could I have been so wrong about Fitz? Because he was friendly and looked the part of the good-natured owner? I'd judged him A-Okay the first day I met him, the same way I'd judged the Langhornes shallow and stuck-up. I'd even judged B.C. guilty of everything.

"You won't get away with this!" I cried. "I'll tell everything!"

Fitz's smile looked so genuine, with a touch of sadness to it. "They won't believe you, Scoop.

Don't you know that by now?"

Fitz turned back to Storm and raised the syringe, as if he intended to go through with it. "We're in this together, Charley. We have our reputation to think about. This is the last of it. Once the insurance pays off on both horses, we'll be out of debt and in the money."

"Don't!" Charley shouted, grabbing for the needle.

"No!" I screamed.

The stall door swung back, and B.C. stood in the doorway, the whistle between his lips. He blew, but no sound came out.

Suddenly Storm reared, knocking Fitz backwards. The needle fell from his hand as he crashed to the ground. Storm was going crazy trying to get out of the stall. I slipped to the back of the stall and opened the door that led to the pasture. Storm pivoted on her back hooves and burst through the door, galloping full speed to the pasture.

"What did you do, B.C.?" I asked, rushing back to him.

"I blew Charley's whistle like he does. That's what I brought you to the barn to see—Charley and his whistle and the fire stick."

Confused, I turned to Charley. "What's he talking about, Charley?"

Fitz hadn't gotten up off the ground. He sat in the straw, his head in his hands. Charley stood over him. "I wanted Storm to win," Charley said quietly. "I wanted Storm to win for you, Dad. That's why I did it. I would have done anything to give you a winner, to be a winner for you." He let out one loud laugh that gave me chills. "Like father like son, huh, Dad?"

Charley turned to me. "It's called an adrenaline rush, Scoop," he explained, his words sharp as knives. "I've been coming to Storm's stall, lighting a stick and holding it in her face while I blow that whistle. It's a high-frequency whistle. Nobody heard it when I blew the whistle at the track, but Storm sure did. That's when she made that surge in the home stretch. Remember that?"

I remembered. And I remembered B.C. in the truck talking about Charley's whistle. I'd ignored him then too. B.C. hadn't burned those sticks. It was Charley all along.

Charley turned back to his dad. "I'm going out now and find my horse. And when I find her, I'm taking her home. Tonight. I don't want to race Storm any more." He left through the same door Storm had and disappeared into the pasture.

B.C. and I left Mr. Fitzsimmons on the stall floor, all alone. I walked home with my brother, feeling closer to him than I ever had. I felt like I knew the real B.C. better too, the amazing person God had created, the one who got lost unless I bothered to look deeper.

The next morning, when I went back to Horsefeathers, every trace of the Fitzsimmonses and their horses was gone—all except a lingering sense of Melly that I couldn't get out of my heart.

Later Travis and Jen helped me write letters to the racing stewards at County Downs, telling them everything and leaving the investigation in their hands. I had a feeling it would be a long time before the Fitzsimmons green silks would be showing up on the racing circuit.

That night I called a special meeting of Horsefeathers and invited Travis, Ray, and B.C. to come too. We crammed into the small office in the barn, where Carla sat on Ray's lap and the rest of us found room on the floor or on the desk. I went over the whole story with everybody, especially the part where B.C. saved the day. I had to fight off tears every time I mentioned Melly's name. I would never forget that horse as long as I lived.

"I don't care if I ever see another race horse again!" declared Maggie 37.

"Is it time for new business yet?" Carla asked. She hadn't said much during the meeting, not even one I told you so.

"The floor is yours," I said.

"Good. I think I may have some more business for us," she said.

"Great!" Jen said, always glad to hear where

the next nickel was coming from.

"I have these acquaintances who own several rodeo horses. They'd like to board some here for—"

"No way!" I cried. "Rodeo horses?"

Carla grinned. "Just kidding."

The meeting adjourned, and we automatically drifted to our horses. I don't know whose idea it was, but in a few minutes we were all mounted for a moonlight ride. Jen, Travis, and Maggie were on their own horses. Ray and Carla rode double on Ham, and B.C. and I rode Orphan.

Behind me I felt the pressure of my little brother's chest against my back, his small arms around my waist, as Orphan led our Horsefeathers herd out into the night. We rode beneath the stars, through fields where the horse music of hooves and God's creation flowed as naturally as moonlight—and the only racing was in my heart.

Glossary of Racing Terms

Also Eligible: A horse that may legally be entered into a race, but will only race if another horse has to drop out.

Also Ran: Any horse that doesn't finish first, second, or third in a race.

Bleeder: A horse that bleeds during heavy exertion, usually from blood vessels involved in the respiratory system.

Break: The starting charge out of the gate as the race begins.

Call: The play-by-play description of the race by the announcer.

Chalk: The favorite horse in a particular race, the one most bet on.

Claiming Race or Claim's Stake: A race where horses are entered according to the price set on them for purchase. Horses may be bought before the race at the claiming price.

Clubhouse Turn: Usually considered the final turn on a race track, just before the homestretch.

Colt: A male horse under 4 years.

Filly: A female horse under 4 years.

Furlong: Measure used on most race tracks; one furlong = one-eighth of a mile.

Green: An inexperienced horse, or one that's immature.

Homestretch: The straight track that stretches from the final turn to the finish line.

Irons: Stirrups

Lead Pad: A special saddle pad with pockets to hold weights and even horses' loads for a race.

Maiden: A horse of either sex that has not won a race.

Mudder: A race horse that runs best when the track is muddy and sloppy.

Paddock: The area where horses are saddled before a race.

Place: Come in second place in a race, behind the winner.

Post: The starting gate.

Position or Post Position: The position in the starting gate, numbered from the inside spot. Places are determined by lottery.

Scratch: To pull a horse out of a race before the start.

Shed Row: The barn area at the track.

Show: Come in third in a race.

Silks: A stable's colors; the jockey's jacket and cap.

Sound: In good shape; no physical problems.

Steward: A racing official who is responsible for seeing that horses and people comply with racing laws and proper conduct. Generally, racetracks have three stewards.

Tack: A horse's equipment, as saddle and bridle.

Tote Board: The large board in the infield of a race track that provides racing information and betting odds and figures, as well as winners (win, place, show) of each race, along with their times.

About the Author

Dandi Daley Mackall rode her first horse—bareback when she was 3. She's been riding ever since. She claims some of her best friends have been horses she and her family have owned: mixed-breeds, quarter horses, American Saddle Horses, Appaloosas, Pintos, and Paints.

When she isn't riding, Dandi is writing. She has published more than 200 books for children and adults, including *The Cinnamon Lake Mysteries* and *The Puzzle Club Mysteries*, both for Concordia. Dandi has written for *Western Horseman* and other magazines as well. She lives in rural Ohio, where she rides the trails with her husband Joe (also a writer), children Jen, Katy, and Dan, and the real Moby and Cheyenne (pictured above).

Photo by Brad Ruebensaal